# Flames

Robbie Arnott was born in Launceston in 1989. His writing has appeared in numerous magazines and anthologies. He won the 2015 Tasmanian Young Writers' Fellowship and the 2014 Scribe Non-fiction Prize for Young Writers. He lives in Hobart.

# Flames

## Robbie Arnott

atlantic · *fiction*

First published in Australia by The Text Publishing Company Pty Ltd, 2018.

First published in hardback in Great Britain in 2018 by Atlantic Books,
an imprint of Atlantic Books Ltd.

This paperback edition published in 2019.

10 9 8 7 6 5 4 3 2 1

A CIP catalogue record for this book is available from the British Library.

Paperback ISBN: 978 1 78649 629 4
E-book ISBN: 978 1 78649 627 0

Printed and bound in Great Britain by Clays Ltd, Elcograf S.p.A.

Atlantic Books
An imprint of Atlantic Books Ltd
Ormond House
26–27 Boswell Street
London
WC1N 3JZ

www.atlantic-books.co.uk

*For Alex White*

The western clouds divided and subdivided themselves into pink flakes modulated with tints of unspeakable softness; and the air had so much life and sweetness, that it was a pain to come within doors.

*Ralph Waldo Emerson, 'Nature'*

# ASH

Our mother returned to us two days after we spread her ashes over Notley Fern Gorge. She was definitely our mother—but, at the same time, she was not our mother at all. Since her dispersal among the fronds of Notley, she had changed. Now her skin was carpeted by spongy, verdant moss and thin tendrils of common filmy fern. Six large fronds of tree fern had sprouted from her back and extended past her waist in a layered peacock tail of vegetation. And her hair had been replaced by cascading fronds of lawn-coloured maidenhair—perhaps the most delicate fern of all.

This kind of thing wasn't uncommon in our family.

Our grandmother had reappeared a few days after her ashes were scattered into the north-facing strait at Hawley

Beach. She'd been sporting a skirt of cowrie shells, a fish hook in her tongue, skin of shifting sand, strands of kelp for hair and a large greenlip abalone suckered onto the back of her neck as she approached a group of terrified fishermen, her wrinkled arms outstretched and the sound of crashing waves swirling out of her salt-rimmed mouth. Our great-aunt Margaret had also returned, not long after her ashes had been poured over the family farm down at Bothwell. When she'd wandered back into her living room she immediately started shedding sheets of paperbark all over the carpet, while an ornate crown of bluegum branches burst from her head and the furred tail of a Bennett's wallaby flopped out from beneath her dress. And our cousin Ella had been spotted a week after her ashes were given to the high scraping winds of Stacks Bluff. With a speckled body of dolerite and an iced face of hard sky she strode into her former school and marched slowly through the grounds, leaving a trail of snapped frost behind each fallen step.

There were others, too—aunts and cousins and ancestors fused with leaf and lichen, root and rock, feather and fur. It had been happening for generations, ever since our ancestors had come to the island, or maybe even longer; nobody seemed to know. The only sure thing was the ratio: around a third of the McAllister women returned to the family after they'd been cremated. The men never did.

They all had their own reasons for returning—unfinished business, old grudges, forgotten chores. Once they'd done what they came back for they trudged back to the

2

landscape that had re-spawned them, and we never saw them again.

Our mother came back for four days. My sister, Charlotte, and I guessed that it had something to do with our father, who hadn't spoken to any of us in years, but our mother didn't give anything away. On the first day she showered for six hours. Like real ferns, her leafy appendages required a lot of moisture. On the second day she limited herself to a two-hour shower and wandered around the house, trailing her delicate fronds across family photos and heirlooms, ignoring Charlotte and me as we tried to talk to her. On the third she stopped showering altogether. And on the fourth she walked out the front door, smiled at the winter sun and hiked for a full day to our father's house, where she waited on his lawn for him to find her.

By the time he did she'd been without water for two days. Her foliage was brown, cracked and dust-dry. As our father walked towards her she began vigorously rubbing two of her large tree-fern fronds together. When he was within speaking distance a thin curl of smoke began rising from her back. And when he reached out to touch her mossy face a crackled lick of fire spread up, over and through her. He recoiled, falling backwards as her body swarmed with flames and she burned, fast and bright and loud, blood-orange in the night.

Δ

While this event upset us—and I guess our father as well, although I can't be certain—I quickly got over it. Everyone

3

dies, even when they're reincarnated. But Charlotte struggled to move on. The black patch of burnt grass in our father's lawn glued itself into her mind. I began to find her staring at the forest, touching plants, sniffing rocks, licking trees. Currawong calls would draw her down into the gullies that carved through our property. Whale spray, rising from the nearby ocean, threw her into fits of uncontrolled screaming. I wondered what form she would take when she returned to me, which brought thoughts of our mother, burning to ash for the second time.

These thoughts proved endless, and worrying, and terrible, and the more Charlotte struggled the more I worried; so I did what I thought was right. I started looking for a coffin, and I swore to bury her whole and still and cold.

# SALT

The sand was hard and sharp and blowing up into Karl's shins, whipped cruel by the dead northerly coming in over the white-chopped sea. He increased his pace, trotting across the beach, juggling his bucket and tackle box and rod, heading for the boatsheds and the trail that lay between them, the one that curled through the boobialla and up to the smoky heat of his house and lounge and family.

His haul: two blackbacks and three lizards, dragged from the water near the salt-pocked pylons of the old jetty, the one that rotted around the turn of the Hawley headland. Each fish killed by a smack of Karl's knifepoint between the eyes. Some people nicked the gills and left them to bleed out in a bucket of seawater. Others filleted them alive, sliding fillets off wriggling spines. And some left them to drown in the air, gills pumping, scales darkening. But a well-aimed strike to the brain is the fastest way to render a fish dead, and this was how Karl did it, with speed and precision and an absence of feeling.

Yet this—this standing on a rock, casting, waiting; slow breathing, glum patience, big stillness—this wasn't fishing. Not really. This was angling. Fishing, as far as Karl was concerned, happened out over the break of the waves and in the rolling navy, bobbing high and steady with a spear in one hand and the slick scruff of a seal in the other, waiting for the run of a beast more weapon than fish: the Oneblood tuna. A man couldn't hunt it alone, and neither could a seal, but together they could kill a beast twice as heavy as the two of them combined. Men from the north coast of this southern island—muttering men, salt-rinsed men, men like Karl—had been hunting this way since before records of the coast were kept. Each hunter formed a bond in their youth with a pup they would seek out from the rocky colonies offshore. Here, past the narrow heads that sheltered Hawley and its neighbouring towns from the wider strait, the seals hauled out on the narrow ledges of a few rock spires that rose from the sea, jostling for space amid gull guano and mussels. In spring the young northmen would row out to them, leaving their soft beaches and dappled bluegums to seek out a hunting companion; or more than that, if they believed their own myths: to find the half of themselves they had been born without.

Karl's seal was a New Zealand fur pup he'd locked eyes with while swaying in the slimy touch of a kelp forest. Their connection had been sharp and sudden: Karl diving from his dinghy, stroking across a reef to the kelp, then stopped by a head that emerged a metre in front of him. Two black orbs glowed out of the smooth brown dome with a heaviness that Karl had never known, and he had reached, without thinking, offering his hand for the pup to sniff or lick or maul. After what had felt like a whole season the pup leaned in to his grip and rested a slippery cheek and a comb of wiry whiskers against the lines of Karl's palm. Their staring continued. The pup grunted. Karl, now exhausted by furious water-treading, reached out with his free hand to cup the pup's other cheek. The ocean rolled into his mouth as he sucked upwards at the low sky. The seal rested, the waves chopped, and the true meaning of salt and water and air wobbled inside Karl's mind. And just as a blinding curtain of sting-water bobbed over his eyes the seal barked, jumped and flashed away into the underwater forest. Karl flopped back to his dinghy, drowned-rat wet and sore and numb, with no idea if it had worked, if he would ever see the pup again, if he'd done anything at all.

But two days later he moored his dinghy on a buoy out near the gushing current of the strait, lifted his grandfather's spear and looked out over the big-blown waves to see the pup, flippers in the air, eyes boring once again into his own. Karl sucked air and dived headfirst into the swell, kicked his flippers hard and headed for the tuna grounds—and with each double-kick of his skinny legs he followed the twirling, back-and-forthing figure of his fur seal.

In their first year together they learned little and caught nothing. They were too young, small and inexperienced to take down a Oneblood—which weigh, on average, around four hundred and fifty kilograms. The most they could do was swim to where the fish congregated and watch them feed on kingfish and salmon, their huge barrelled bodies torpedoing through the water, scales shining, jaws lunging. To behold a Oneblood is to gaze upon a manifestation of strength and purpose that no human, no matter how gifted or determined, will ever even approach. A creature this large, this heavy, this wrapped in bulging muscle, should be slug-gish; yet a Oneblood can fly through saltwater at over one hundred kilometres an hour. A fish this strong should hunt by force; but no, a Oneblood would rather sneak and pounce than rip and roar. A beast this mighty should be impossible to miss; but a Oneblood is camouflaged by the murk of the ocean, only appearing when it cares to be witnessed.

Hanging in the ocean, Karl saw the Onebloods appear from the depths as if through a portal: dark blueness one second, a missile of muscle and scales the next, rising up after its prey at a speed so fast the water boiled around its body. And then, with its quarry captured, it was gone—zipped back into the darker depths. Seeing one hunt was tricky enough; to Karl, killing one seemed impossible. But he knew it could be done—he had seen them brought back on Hawley boats since he was a child, mountains of ruby flesh with a long spear protruding from the thick, purple-red artery that ran from their throat to their dorsal and gave the species its name.

His seal seemed to have no doubt they could do it. In that first year he joined Karl on every expedition, flicking his fast, sleek body around Karl's bobbing limbs as they watched the Onebloods feed. Sometimes he chased a tuna for twenty or thirty metres, but always broke off and returned to Karl, a doggish smile hanging from his whiskers. With no tuna meat to hand he fed on squid and salmon, slowly growing in weight and girth and strength. Karl kept himself alive by working as a decky on a fishing charter, helping smooth-gripped tourists drag in snapper, couta and some of the smaller tuna varieties, such as bluefin or albacore—beasts that were to Onebloods as house cats are to jaguars. It was after one of these trips, while depositing some lawyers back on the docks at Hawley, that Karl saw the McAllister matriarch rising from the tide, reborn, bedecked with cowries, sand-skin and a large abalone stuck to her neck. Karl didn't take much notice; McAllister women, he'd always been told, were trouble, whether they breathed with lungs or gills or not at all.

After work, after helping his parents around the house, Karl was always back out in the water with his seal. In their second year together they began making half-hearted chases after juvenile Onebloods. His seal now weighed eighty kilograms, and would feint and slip after the tuna in a twitchy dance that their supposed prey would largely ignore. Karl ignored him too, for the most part, until the day his seal flipped back to him with a single glimmering scale clenched in his mouth. Three weeks later he drew blood; a mid-sized Oneblood shot away from them leaking a thin trail of iron-rich redness, and the seal could barely move his jaws for days after nipping at such a ferocious force of movement.

In their third year they began choreographing the moves that every tuna team must master. First, the seal must pick up the flashing premonition of the Oneblood as it surges from the depths. Then he must dive below the great fish and begin to harass it, through a series of turns, nips, circles and feints. A Oneblood is faster than any seal over a straight line, but in short angles its massive bulk can't keep up. Corralled in this way the Oneblood will seek to catch the seal and rip the irritating mammal into hot pieces. When it can't, its next move will be to escape, and it is then that the seal must really get to work. As the fish looks for an easy exit the seal must herd it upwards, gradually, patiently, towards the stabs of sunlight and the wind-cut surface and the waiting spear of his partner.

By now the Oneblood is uncomfortable, furious and, probably for the first time in its life, afraid. Since the seal has begun its corral the fish has not been in control of its movements, and it does not like this: not at all. Most of all it hates the seal—in the same way humans hate the whine of a mosquito that fizzes past the ear just as they are tumbling into sleep—so it does not even notice the dangling legs of its other hunter, nor the gleaming barb of its weapon.

When fish and seal have come within three metres of the sea's lid it is time for the human to act. And it is not hard, really, not when compared with what the seal has done, but it takes precision, and speed, and a certain calmness. As the Oneblood reaches striking distance the paddling hunter must dive beneath the surface, ready his aim, wait for the flash of the fish's white underbelly and, most importantly, the purple seam of life that threads through its body. When the artery is visible he must strike. He cannot miss, not even by an inch, because a spear plunged into scales and muscle will no more annoy the tuna than the nips of the seal, and it will escape. The point and barb of the spear must cannon into the glowing artery, where the scales are thin and the life is beating. Blood will cloud the sea, and the eyes and mouth of the Oneblood will yank wide.

Now arrives the hardest part of the hunter's job: holding on. As its life-juice leaks away the tuna begins to thrash with all the strength and panic stored up in its mighty body, and the hunter must not let go of his spear; he must remain connected to his prey, even as he is torqued and whipped through the water like a kite in a storm, even as the air is shaken out of his lungs in big rush-rising bubbles. It is only when this wild thrashing slows down—which could take two, three, five minutes—that the watching seal flies in to clamp a hard mouth onto the spine at the back of the Oneblood's head, crunching down on the brain stem; and finally, out of blood, out of mind, the great fish dies, and the exhausted seal and drowning hunter must drag it to the boat, where it is gaffed and winched aboard before sharks sniff the blood and bring more, unwanted death.

This process is easy to describe, much harder to carry out. During that third year Karl and his seal attempted it dozens of times, never getting close to making a kill, usually coming much closer to being killed themselves by their harried, huge prey. More happened in this year—Karl's parents gave up on coastal life and moved to a unit down south in the capital, leaving the family cottage to Karl with the proviso that he occasionally visited them; his seal swelled to one hundred kilos and began to grow a thick mane around his scruff; a storm smashed up the fishing boat Karl worked on, robbing him of three months' wages; and when it was repaired, on their first charter with a group of tourism-industry bigwigs, he met Louise.

Early on there was talk that he'd move across to Devonport, where she ran her holiday-booking business, but this idea never caught on. (Karl only went along with it out of courtesy; he knew that Hawley had hooked her.) When Louise realised there was no uprooting Karl she moved herself into the cottage, bringing her business with her and turning the spare room into an office. Karl, by now in his late twenties, felt an itch beneath the salt on his skin when he started seeing her on his shabby deck every evening as he trudged home, and knew, even though he had never spoken to anyone about women or courting or even the reddening notion of love, that he needed to do something permanent about her. He knew it as surely as he knew the Hawley tides—but it wasn't all up to him.

For the final approval he goaded Louise into his dinghy,

muttering not much at all in response to her questions, and chugged out to the spires beyond the heads. Here he raised his spear, as he always did, and within a minute his seal joined them. He splashed Karl with both fore-flippers, eager to hunt, but stopped when he saw Louise. A heavy stare. A long blink. A slow, submerged circumnavigation of the boat. A re-emergence and a querulous bark. Louise baulked. *Reach for him*, Karl asked. *Please.* After a few moments of hesitation she did, looking back and forth between Karl and the seal, not panicked, but certainly not comfortable. The seal splashed, barked louder, and moved in. The heat of its breath stank across her knuckles. The seal's mouth opened, revealing small, bright-white daggers. Its head dipped, rolled, twisted…and then it was butting her hand, turning it over, revealing the thin, vulnerable skin of her wrist and the blue veins shining through it. Her eyes shot circular and she nearly yanked back her arm, but Karl said: *Wait, wait. Let him come.* Against all her instincts she did, with her eyes closed, so she didn't see the seal swim an inch closer and lean his face against her palm; she only felt it. At his touch her eyes opened, and she looked down to see the resting watery face throwing a heavy stare up at her. *Now your other hand*, said Karl. *Use both.* And just as he had done years earlier, she moved in and cupped the seal's head, now far larger than when Karl had first held it. The moment lingered. A contented bark leapt from his hot mouth and then, with a diving flip, he was gone, leaving Louise to shriek with relief and wonder, and turn to Karl and see two trails of hot water running down his cheeks, mixing salt with salt.

13

Three months later a sharp-cut diamond was bouncing light off her finger, paid for by the first Oneblood that Karl and his seal caught.

After the kill Karl had lain prone in the boat, sucking in gulps of air, rubbing the ruff of his seal as it dozed against his leg. The hunt had gone more or less the way it was meant to: a smooth shepherd, a tight breath, a true strike. Steel met blood in a jagged rupture, and Karl had just held on to the shaft as his bones were jiggled by their writhing, dying prey. When the seal had crunched into the spine and the fish went limp Karl was so surprised he almost forgot what they were meant to do next. Pushing, heaving and winching the Oneblood into the boat had drained all the strength they had left.

Now he floated under a pale sun. The sky was half wiped with the fluff and cream of clouds, but enough yolky heat was leaking down onto his tired limbs to keep him from shivering. His other half lay sleeping beside him. Their victim lay glassy-eyed and still-gilled. Thoughts were flicking through Karl's mind, not holding, running away from him before coherence caught up. He dropped one hand into his partner's ruff and lifted the other upwards. A warm breeze brushed against this risen hand, a breeze carrying tang and salt and the clearing scent of eucalyptus as he clenched his fingers around wet, warm fur.

∆

He sold the Oneblood meat to a Japanese wholesaler named Oshikawa for an amount of money that made his head swim in ways that no fish or seal ever could. Oshikawa had wanted the whole animal, guts and head and all, but Karl had laughed—those parts belonged to the seal, and everyone in the fish industry knew it (including the seal, who wolfed down his share on the dock in front of a troop of delighted schoolchildren). With the money he had bought Louise's ring; and a month later they caught another Oneblood, selling it to the same wholesaler for an even higher price. After their third catch he quit his job on the charter boat and dedicated every working day of the season to the tuna grounds.

In the next year they caught four fish, and the season after they brought in six. This proved to be their average number over the next decade: six fat, fierce, fighting Oneblood tuna, sometimes as few as three, occasionally as many as ten. The seal stopped growing at one hundred and sixty kilograms, but he didn't lose any of his zip, and at his full weight and strength he could herd up the largest Onebloods going around, giving Karl—whose spear arm had become reliably accurate—the unenviable task of holding on to the violent death throes of a furious six-hundred-kilo fish.

Their victories in the water were matched by Louise's success on land. The tourism industry around the north coast thrived, and after a couple of years she was able to rent an office in town, allowing them to turn her home office into a nursery, which was soon occupied by their first daughter. Eighteen months later another daughter appeared, and amid all this swimming and spearing, earning and child-rearing,

Karl noticed that they were getting older, all of them, and he didn't mind anywhere near as much as he thought he would have.

Eventually he retired—much sooner than he had planned to. But he retired, nonetheless; why else would he now be trudging along a windy beach, carrying tiny, line-caught fish that a Oneblood wouldn't even bother to nibble? It wasn't his choice; it wasn't his idea; but the salt and waves held other plans for him.

It came about on a clear day, with a hard blue smear of sky shining above his boat, a perfect day for being in the water. A normal start: half an hour of floating until the tuna began to bullet upwards after the pilchard swarms, then a few false chases before his seal ran a ring around a big male. The corral was seamless, and Karl's spear had shot true. The shake and bite and blood cloud had all been uncomplicated, and the kill was completed in a routine manner. It was only as they were hauling the fish towards the moored dinghy that Karl felt something go wrong. It was not a mental feeling, no gut twinge or rumbly sense of fear—it was physical, a feeling of something huge and powerful bumping into his hip as it slid past him through the water.

His first thought: shark. But he knew, even before he turned around, that this wasn't a shark; the bumping weight had been wrapped in smooth, rubbery skin, not the rasping cartilage of shark hide. Swivelling in the water, still not seeing the creature, his ears were filled with a rapid rhythm of clicks and high-pitched squeaks. And finally, after a full three-hundred-and-sixty-degree turn, he saw it, in all its fins and flukes and black-and-white immensity: an orca.

The seal had swum to his side and was watching the whale double back. Karl wasn't worried, not initially. Orcas don't attack humans, and a single one won't go after a full-grown fur seal—twisting agility and sharp teeth make it too risky a meal. It probably just wanted their tuna. Karl pushed the dead fish towards it and started back-paddling towards the boat. But the orca ignored the carcass, pushing it aside with a nudge of its tail—and then a second clicking song thrummed through the water. The seal flipped around faster than Karl could move, as a second orca wafted past them on the left. A third approached them from the right and a fourth—dark, fast, its click song a jittering swarm of sound—swam directly beneath them. They peeled off to join the circling movements of their pod mates. Now the orcas were whirlpooling around them, and the seal was spinning around Karl even faster, trying to keep eyes on them all. Karl clutched his spear. His pulse tripped staccato.

And then: relentless and inevitable, it began. Each orca took turns barrelling towards the seal from a different direction, breaking off its charge at the last minute as the seal turned and showed its teeth. Karl followed the orcas with the point of his spear, keeping it outstretched towards them, but they started charging in weaves; he couldn't keep up. The seal couldn't run—they would catch it over a straight line—but it wasn't trying to escape. With each aborted charge it moved closer to Karl, spinning around him, and Karl realised he was being protected, even though the orcas were not hunting him.

And then, in his right periphery, he saw the rushing gape of a glossy pink maw. He lurched in the cold wet and aimed his spear forward, as his seal bobbed in front of him, lips bared, muscles coiled. He thrust the spear and missed by metres, miles, oceans, as the orca baulked, and the tiny bounce of relief that hung in his stomach was overtaken by a vast swell that rushed him backwards, followed by an even bigger thwack of rubber and muscle. He was tossing now, overturning and disoriented, only just seeing the fluke of a different orca that had risen beneath him and sent him somersaulting through the water.

After two full revolutions his body stopped flipping. He regained his bearing and cracked his head through the surface, sucking in air before diving back below. He couldn't see his seal. He couldn't see the orcas either, but he could still hear their clicking songs. He swivelled and spun and swam in every direction, left right up down north south, but there was nothing but bubbles and navy and clicks.

But then another noise intruded—a harsh slap that sounded like it had come from above the water, not through it. Karl surfaced. First he saw nothing; but from behind his head he heard the slap again, so he turned, and there he saw it. He saw it happening through his waterlogged, salt-reddened eyes. He saw it sped up and slowed down. He saw his seal's body being slammed against the water by the orcas. They took turns gripping its tail in their teeth and flinging their heads left to right, over and over again, using the hard lid of the ocean to break Karl's seal into ragged chunks of brown-red meat.

Δ

In the months between the orca attack and his walk down the beach, clenching his teeth against the grit blowing into his shins, Karl tried to forget that clicking sound. But it was lodged in a hole between his ears, a backdrop to his days that he feared and hated but could not escape. He was reminded of it constantly: when a light switch was flicked, when Louise clicked her fingers, when his leaping daughters clicked their heels, when Sharon at the fish-and-chip shop clicked her tongue against the roof of her mouth as she waited for the oil in the deep fryer to heat up. All these humdrum sounds and more stirred up the bouncing echolocation of the orcas, and with them came the images, and the memory of the warm salt breeze, and the slapping crack of his seal as its body was broken against the ocean's face.

He didn't find another seal; he didn't even try. He knew of other hunters who had successfully re-partnered, but he didn't have the energy or appetite to start the training process all over again. And the idea of seeking out a fresh pup raised bile in his throat—it made his own seal swim up through his memories, resting its young face against his palm. And then the clicks would return, haunting snaps that floated through the water endlessly towards him, and Karl would mash thumbs into his ears or take a chainsaw to a bluegum or gargle rum until one of his daughters found him hacking dry sobs at the bay.

Perhaps this abandonment of the hunt was a good thing. He started hearing rumours that the Oneblood stocks were declining. At first he thought the other fishermen were lying, trying to drag his spirits up from the seabed, but then a story appeared in the paper that was headlined 'Worst Tuna Season in Decade'.

He spoke to his old wholesaler, the fastidious Oshikawa, who confirmed the report. *Bad year*, he told Karl over a pint of stout. *Not many fish, and the fish I have seen are small.* Karl lapped at the creamy tide of his dinner and Oshikawa, fingering a coaster, said: *Maybe a disease we haven't picked up. Maybe a monsoon somewhere messed up the food chain. Maybe the water is getting warmer.* He tore the coaster into white flecks. *Maybe just a bad season.* Karl sipped, fiddled with his own coaster and was about to ask a question, but as he opened his mouth someone closed the pub door, and the latch shouted out a loud, clear click that forced Karl to change the subject.

Money was no problem. Years of catching and killing Onebloods had left him with what many people would call a small fortune, certainly enough to pay for the groceries, insurance, even to send his daughters to a private boarding school in Launceston. Louise was still pulling in a decent income, so there was no need for him to go back to work on the charter boats. He knew he needed to do something to keep himself occupied, but all he knew was swell and spear and seal.

So: the family went on holidays, up and down the rocky peaks and dipping valleys of the island. They spent a long weekend in a former hydro factory in the highlands. For five days they wandered up and down the frosty crags of Cradle Mountain, sleeping in a roomy stone cabin owned by Oshikawa. They ate abalone, hammered tender before their eyes, on a wharf at Stanley. Louise took them to the glistening greenness of Notley Fern Gorge, west to the dark moonland of the Queenstown hills, and to the wren-blue tide of Boat Harbour, where Karl dragged his toes through the surf but didn't wade past the depth of his knees. They went south, almost as far south as they could, down to the wide wilds of Melaleuca. Their younger daughter grew bored and sullen, but the older one—Nicola, recently turned eighteen, soon to begin studying at veterinary school—became so wide-eyed and enamoured with the place that she didn't want to leave. Karl tried to match her enthusiasm, but he couldn't feel what his daughter's soul was touching. He hiked white quartzite mountains and watched wombats stumble and stared out at the green buttongrass plains at this southern end of the world, and though he smiled at Louise and the girls (and even occasionally laughed) all he saw through the grass was a seal hitting the sea, and all he heard in this high empty sky was a pulsing rhythm of underwater clicks.

Back at home the girls showed no interest in hunting Onebloods. Instead, he taught them to push hooks through frozen squid and hurl them out into the water, which they loved as much as he found it boring. And through sharing

21

this banal activity with his daughters he somehow developed an affection for the activity itself, and found himself angling off the rocks even when the girls were away in Devonport, casting and catching and occasionally crying, but only when the mist was clear and he could see past the heads towards the tall spires where the seals still hauled out, or so he assumed.

Δ

This was how angling put Karl on the beach on that windy evening, feeling the whipped sand feast on his shins. Soon he would figure out what to do next. Soon the clicks would stop, and he would stop hearing his seal hit the sea, and an idea or direction or purpose would swim up at him. The wind hammered. He kept trudging into the sand.

As he neared his cottage he saw a young man riffling through a clump of driftwood. He was not quite six feet tall, with milky skin and sharply dark hair. Underfed angles jutted out from his chin, cheeks, collarbone. He held a long white-grey branch in his hands, lifting it with difficulty to his eyes, which bored deep into the pattern of the barkless wood. His arms looked even more malnourished than his face.

*Evening*, Karl mumbled as he passed. The young man said nothing but turned around, transferring the intensity of his stare from the branch to Karl's face. Karl stopped. *Nice branch.*

*I thought so*, the young man said, *but no. It's not right.* Karl looked up at the light he could see blinking from his deck and thought about walking straight there, getting out of the wind and away from this odd stranger, but small-town courtesy compelled him to pause. *Not right for what?*

The young man swivelled the branch in his hand and ran his free fingers up and down its knobbly length. *For a coffin.*

Karl felt surprise creep into his brow, but kept it out of his voice. *Not gonna make much of a coffin with driftwood, mate.*

*No.* The man sighed. *I suppose not.* He underarmed the branch onto the sand and bent over to resume picking through its siblings.

Again Karl glanced up at his cottage, its light, its promise of warmth and food and Louise. *Mate, do you need any help?*

*Pardon?* He didn't look up.

*I mean. I dunno.* Karl exhaled. *Is everything okay?* The young man straightened up with a quizzical expression on his face, as if Karl was the one behaving strangely. Karl extended a hand. *I'm Karl.*

He accepted Karl's palm in his own. *Levi.* And then, as if his surname was an afterthought: *McAllister.* He let go and ran his hand through his hair. *Everything's fine.*

*Righto.* The name bumped around between Karl's ears where the clicks usually lived. *I'm sorry.*

The quizzical expression reappeared on the young man's face. *What about?*

*This coffin. Your loss.*

Now a smile spread across the sunken, youthful cheeks. *Oh. No. Nobody has died. Well, not recently.* He waved at the pile of wood as if that explained something. *I'm just getting things ready for my sister.*

*Is she sick?*

*No.*

Karl's bouncing thoughts snagged—the name: McAllister. His eyebrows came together; he knew how things went. He'd seen one of them climb from the water, beshelled and undead, back when he was young and his seal was half-grown. He knew about the flames, and he knew what happened next, and he heard himself ask: *How old is she?*

The wind died, as if blown out like a candle, and the stinging sand fell to the beach as Levi McAllister peered into Karl's bucket to stare at the still gills of the dry, head-stabbed fish. *She's twenty-three.*

# SKY

Charlotte is running. She is a jangle of loose limbs and hitting heels as she sprints down the driveway, gravel spitting from her steps, the dusk darkening above her. Her breaths are jagged; her shoes are biting; her eyes are clouded.

Charlotte is running because a few hours earlier she was reading, in the dim light of their lounge, a book her brother had left on the coffee table: *The Wooden Jacket*, by Thurston Hough. A book about tree care, she had thought, or cabinetry, or even fashion, until she peeled back the cover and saw the pictures: pictures of coffins. Simple coffins with straight blond slats; wide coffins that blinked with gloss; enormous sarcophagi with ornate detailing and velvet interiors. Odd, she thought, until she found the notepad next to the book.

This notepad—yellow, blue-lined, covered with the neat marks of Levi's hand—contained a series of measurements.

*172 cm*
*58 – 62 kg*
*Size 8 (dress)*

Familiar numbers, but she wasn't sure where from. But then—a flicker of intuition. She ran her hands up and down her forearms. She pulled at the part of her jumper that cinched in against her waist. She remembered her mother reaching up to scratch a notch into the hallway above her head when she was seventeen. She looked from the measurements to the book, back to the measurements, and then back to the coffins upon coffins that filled her brother's book. And then Charlotte was wobbling on her feet, her blood was pounding against her wrists, her mother was burning behind her eyes, and she was throwing only her favourite and most necessary clothes and possessions into a backpack before reeling out the front door and into the dusk.

Charlotte is gasping, dragging in air as fast and deep as she can. She's reached the end of the driveway and thrown a thumb in the air. She hasn't thought hard about what she's doing, but the need to run is clear and huge. Even if he doesn't mean her any harm. Even if he is only doing some research. Even if he's just curious—she will not stay in a house, not even her mother's house, with a brother who wants to bury her. All she has left of her mother are photos and memories and a family tradition of flames, and she won't let him take them from her. Charlotte will burn, tomorrow or in half a century, but she will burn. And she might return. Though that isn't the point.

Charlotte is waving, flagging down the approaching ute and its driver, a neighbour she knows but not well; and now the driver, this sheep farmer with strained belt and hairy neck, is taking her away from the little farm and towards, towards, towards…somewhere. Anywhere.

Charlotte is thinking: *Will I go to him?* But even before she lets this thought finish she knows that she won't, because if her brother wants her buried, what will her father try to do to her? The idea of him has turned her red and bitter ever since he left them, and the more she thinks about it now, watching the sun set over the dimpled banks of the Tamar through the grimy window of the ute, the more she understands that her opinion of him has not changed. She does not trust her father. The ute curls past Gravelly Beach and the window shows her the peeled tide and oozing mudflats of the river. She will not go to him in his big house on the high cliffs: with its timber walls and splintered ceilings, it is another coffin.

Charlotte is stretching. The farmer has rolled out of the Tamar Valley and deposited her at the Launceston bus terminal, and she is leaning down to grab at her toes, wondering where she is going to sleep, because the sky is now the deepest shade of blue. She doesn't know anyone who lives here. She doesn't have much money. She knows only that she wants to walk the stiffness out of her legs, so she strides out, going nowhere in particular, and before long she is down on

27

a humanless boardwalk by the waterfront.

Charlotte is watching the waters of three rivers meet. The two Esks—one brown and slow, the other churned white—mix into the broad slate Tamar that pushes north, away from Charlotte, through the reedy wetlands. Beneath the water's three-way face swim countless mud eels, but nobody is angling for them from the pontoons that hang onto the river's edge—it is too dark. Earlier the sun would have dipped behind the cliffs of Launceston's craggy gorge, brushing the waterfront with fingers of pale winter light, but now the docks have sunk too deep into the sky's navy for anything to be visible in detail. Charlotte makes out the yellow lights of townhouse windows, twin looming wheat silos, the gaudy curves of Kings Bridge, black trees. Clouds crowd the moon and the navyness intensifies. Charlotte, now unable to see even the border between blunt gorge cliff and dark night sky, wanders to a low dock. Here she lifts the lid of an overturned dinghy and crawls underneath its shell, and minutes later, with a cluster of ropes and nets for a pillow, she swirls into sleep.

Charlotte is dreaming. The thistled fields of her farm are melting into vast squares of green lava, flowing down to the pebbled beach. The gullies that rise up from the beach—the ones she tumbled through as a child, chasing her brother and mother, feeling ferns brush her knees with every wobbly lunge—freeze, shimmer and crack. Somewhere her mother is spraying water onto sunburnt shoulders, and then these shoulders sprout fronds, out of Charlotte's sight, but there, definitely there. A forest raven is cawing, the fronds are crackling, and now Levi is beating his bony little fists against the sandstone cottage walls as he screams, a high cut scream, even though he is always so controlled…and then Charlotte is surging awake into a new, unwelcome day. A crack of light is shining under the edge of the dinghy; other than that it is black, silent and cold—although not completely cold.

Charlotte is feeling a warm weight pushing against her stomach. In the gloom she fumbles her phone from her pocket and turns on its torch. Its bright field of light introduces her to this source of warmth: a ball of brown fur nuzzled against the concave curve of her belly. She unbends her knees. The fur twitches and a bald tail-tip slides out from underneath it, while a snout pokes up, whiskers tensing, dark eyes blinking. A rakali. A swimmer; a feaster; a bright thief; an oversized native water rat. Charlotte waits for it to flee or squeak or bite, but it remains still, sleepily regarding her, even when she lifts the boat and manoeuvres her body out into the morning. The rakali yawns, snaps its mouth shut and curls back to sleep, untroubled, as Charlotte lowers the dinghy and turns to face the stares being thrown her way by a family of doughy tourists on an early walk.

Charlotte is rolling down a new highway in a new ride: a rickety, rust-pocked Redline bus. After leaving the docks she had bought a ticket from a bored teenager at the bus terminal, telling him only that *I want to go south*. The teenager had mumbled back *We can get you as far as Kingston*, so that's the ticket Charlotte bought. Now she watches the green-blond fields whip past, and in the distance she can see the dark dolerite mountains and rising plateaus, hemming in the great plain of the Midlands. It is mid-morning, early winter. Above her an endless unbroken cloud is clotting up the sky, although there is no rain.

Charlotte is sure, as she sees an empty speedway approach and then recede from view, that she is doing the right thing. Talking to Levi would have done zilch; he would've given her the same look he's been giving her ever since their mother died, the look of pity and care and concern spiced with that skinny jut of resolve in his jawline—the jut that meant he would not be changing his mind, no sir, no matter what his unreasonable, uncontrollable sister said or did or thought. Charlotte knows he thinks she's gone crazy—he's been throwing that jutting look at her every time he's caught her sobbing in the gullies, flinching at the wind and throbbing in the fields. This look of judgement. This look of control. This look of *I need to do something; she needs my help*, when really (as far as Charlotte is concerned) he is the one who needs help, because what is she doing but grieving? Their mother has died. What does it matter what form or sound her grief takes? Surely the help, if help ever arrives, should come screaming down towards her spine-straight brother who has shown no sorrow, no pain, no action other than to jut his chin, and plan to bury his own flesh and blood.

Charlotte is sipping a watery lager in a Tunbridge pub. There is something wrong with the bus; the driver said something had happened to the engine or spark plugs or radiator, and that they'd be underway again in the morning. In the meanwhile, he'd told the milling passengers after they creaked into this worn central town, courtesy of the bus company they'd all be staying the night in the only accommodation available: the Tunbridge Standard. Charlotte was momentarily enraged, though she had nowhere to be, in no certain time. But the other passengers had taken the news with weary, bored acceptance, making her think that buses breaking down on the Midlands must not be uncommon. Her anger ebbed, and evaporated when she saw her neat, comfortable room; she did not want to spend another night with her only warmth coming from a water rat.

Charlotte is listening to a pair of miners mutter into their pints. They're sitting a few stools down the bar and pretending they aren't looking at her every now and then, sneaky twisty little looks that she doesn't mind; she just wishes they were honest about it. They're talking about the things they've dug out of the ground: copper, zinc, ore, silver, even gold, all in the smashing winds and rain of the west coast. Charlotte is not interested in the west, but then she hears the compass shift south. There is a tin mine, she hears, as they gurgle words through their slopping beer, in a town at the bottom of the world. It's called Mallacoota or Mantakoopa or Melanoma— Charlotte can't be sure, exactly. But these miners have noticed her noticing; they have felt her ears jump at this southern talk and they are scraping back their chairs and tottering over to her, ruffling hair and straightening high-vis, all *How's it going* and *Mind if we sit* and *Want another drink?*

Charlotte is remembering: men aren't always terrible. The miners are chatting her up in a lazy, innocent way, not asking personal questions, not probing at her short answers, saying *Thank you* and *You're welcome* like they were raised by good stern mothers, and for the first time in weeks she is relaxing. They've figured out that she'd rather let them do the talking, so they are bouncing off each other in a two-man act, one sharp and funny, the other daft and kind. The sharp one has fluffy yellow hair and a dispiriting moustache, the kind of lip fur that makes your skin creep, but the daft one—and he isn't all that daft, really—is tall and quiet and wearing a red beanie that should look terrible with his fluoro-yellow jacket but somehow looks great. At some point, around the third beer they have bought her, Charlotte has placed a hand on his shoulder as she laughs at nothing in particular and he reacts only by smiling shyly in her direction with the right amount of teeth. The bar crowd is leaking out into the night. Soon it will only be Charlotte and these two men. The lager has taken on a bubbling glow in her throat. A clock bangs somewhere, the sharp miner tells a flat joke, and last drinks are called by the aproned, stone-faced barman.

Charlotte is worming her tongue into the mouth of the daft kind miner in the corridor outside her room, where she has him up against the wall. She can't remember how she'd lured him up here, but it hadn't been difficult; as soon as they turned into the dim light of the hallway her hands were on his chest, pushing back, and she was meeting his slow lips with her hot fast mouth. Now, with a bit of hip-writhing encouragement, his hands lower to grasp her arse, and she is lifted up onto the points of her toes. She pushes harder with her hips, feeling him, hard and welcome, and her hands are scrabbling at his scarlet beanie as one of his hands brushes firmly down her arm...but no—no, it doesn't. Both his palms are still gripping the flesh in her jeans. Charlotte untangles their tongues and jerks her neck backwards to see the fuzz of the other miner's lip fur, looming up close to her face. His hand is slithering around her shoulders, fingers firm and the rest of him firming too, his flesh closing off the gap between them. Charlotte looks to the first miner, her miner, and he is smiling that shy smile that she only now realises isn't shy at all. And then he winks, first at his friend, and then at her, and they have done this before; they have rehearsed this; it was their plan all along. But the daft miner's wink—and he truly is daft if he thinks this will work—does something else: it shakes off her shock. She roars back into the physicality of her body and can suddenly feel both of them crowding her, boxing her, four hands swarming all over her, lip fur bristling her ear, and then the soft warm vessel beneath their touch becomes a spinning top of knees and elbows and nails and teeth, and somewhere she feels a burst of heat that blazes for a volcanic moment before disappearing.

Charlotte is shouting *Go fuck yourselves!* to the back-pedalling miners and then *Or just go fuck each other.* She twirls into her room, buzzing with anger and fear and booze as the daft miner clutches his wrist. She can hear them whispering, and she shouts again—no words, just a loud, hard peal of rage. Their footsteps pound as they flee and now she just wants to sleep; this bed has been bought for her, and she will use it to its full pillowy power, but before she does she is writing something down on the complimentary notepad. It's a name she stole from them while they plied her with beer, a name that reverberates through her somersaulting brain, the name of the tin-mine town: Melaleuca.

Charlotte is snoozing, back on the bus heading south, her head jittering against the thin metal frame. Each tiny thwack against the glass sends an orange pulse through her hangover. It is the next morning; the bus was fixed overnight. She did not see the mining duo in tiny, dark Tunbridge when she rose, and she has already forgotten the particulars of what they looked like. (She hasn't forgotten what they did, or how they treated her, but their features, their voices, their grimy little faces have all happily flown from her mind.) Now she huddles her hangover in the red-white bus under a dawning purple sky. As the sun rises on her left she can see the country in better detail. The world outside should be painted with the thickest of greens at this time of year, but it is not—everything has a look of hunger. From the denuded hills to the beige paddocks there is a sense of meagreness, of malnutrition. Only the bunches of hateful gorse are green, and even they are dry. Winter should be lending these farms and forests an uncontrollable lushness. To Charlotte's wobbly eyes, it isn't right. This dryness. This beigeness. But she can't look at the flying fields for very long before she starts to feel sick, so she turns away, eyelids clenched, and tries to sleep.

Charlotte is waking up and blearily noticing the suburbs of the island's capital: how they bunch, how they are squeezed between the wide estuary and the rolling foothills of the city's mountain. She hopes the bus is going to take her straight through this place; she does not want to stop here, where the buildings are tall and the streets are bright and the people swarm. And she is in luck—the bus chugs through the dull grey centre, past the dappled docks (no water rats in sight, not here), and up a four-lane mini-freeway onto an outlet that pours south, ten minutes later, into the satellite town of Kingston. Charlotte's hangover is still there, but it's more of a queasy tang than a throbbing pain. The bus has stopped at a polished station. She can see a yellow beach, and beyond that, over the estuary, lonely hills; but as she steps off the bus this seaside idyll is disturbed by the wafting wind.

Charlotte's neat nostrils are picking up a scent on the breeze: it smells of cleaning products, starch and artificial sweeteners. It is the smell of white-picket fences, of census-friendly families, of collared shirts at church, of people who gossip and chat and tell everyone everything, and she is marching back into the bus station and asking for a ticket that will take her further south. The desk jockey says *The Franklin connection leaves in a half an hour*, so she asks him to point it out on a map, and when his bony knuckle tells her it's another forty kilometres towards the bottom of the earth she buys a ticket. Half an hour later she's on a bus, this one smaller and smoother. She is swooping up hills and plunging into valleys. She is passing orchards and vineyards

35

and forests. The towns are growing smaller; the fields a
glowing greener; the sky is getting bigger. Finally, the knot
her gut begins to loosen.

Charlotte is wandering the main road of Franklin an
thinking to herself, more with pictures and feelings tha
words, that she is getting closer to wherever she needs to b
The weatherboard shops are humble and calm. The peopl
drifting about by the waterfront are quiet and calm. Th
plumes of smoke that curl out of the chimneys are slow an
calm. The wide river beyond the street is steely, placid an
unstoppably...calm. And Charlotte is calm too, just for bein
here. She is so calm she walks into an antique shop and begin
staring at a map. The mossy green ink of the land ends neatl
when it meets the light blue colour of the ocean. She ha
spotted her destination on the edge of Bathurst Harbou
far into the remote forests of the southwest. But there is
problem: while she has found the dot of Melaleuca, there is n
corresponding road that runs in or out of it. Charlotte find
the owner and asks: *Excuse me, but I was wondering how*
*find the road to Melaleuca?* And the shopkeep, surrounded b
her piles of books and furniture and colonial trinkets, say
without looking up: *You can't.*

Charlotte is tapping a fist against the wooden door o
the cabin of a paint-peeling yacht, her calmness having flow
away, up into the winter sky. No sound appears to respond t
her thrumming knuckles, so she taps again, harder, insisten
*No road to Melaleuca*, the antique seller had said. *Boat o*
*plane. Only way in. Only way out.* With a few more question

Charlotte had wheedled out of her the name of the boats that sailed there—or more accurately, the name of this boat, the one she is now attacking with both hands, rap-rap-rap-rap-rap, until finally a belching rumble emanates from inside the hull. The door opens. A face is there. It has grey hair, a grey beard, grey eyes and grey lips covered in strips of skin that are peeling away like the paint on the yacht. Charlotte begins her offer: she will pay, she will work, she will scrub decks, she will clean fish, she will de-cling barnacles and limpets, she will hoist sails and shimmy down masts, if this boat will take her to Melaleuca. The grey man lifts a hand to say something, but Charlotte won't be stopped. She will lasso albatrosses. She will harpoon whales. She will re-paint the yacht whatever colour he likes. She goes on and on and her breathing becomes a ragged, shallow tide, until the grey man yells *Shut up, for god's sake, shut up.* Charlotte stops talking. She is filled suddenly with deep regret: she has stuffed this up. She knows nothing about working on a yacht. She will have to walk through winter to reach Melaleuca. She looks up, staring at the hard fluff of featureless clouds—until a whistle snaps at her ears and her eyes are drawn down to an incoming threat...

Charlotte is reaching out into the air, fingers spread to catch in her palm a long-handled brush that has been thrown her way. The grey man sniffs at her shoes, her clothes, her backpack, and says: *We leave tomorrow morning.*

# IRON

The Esk God yawned at the sudden burn of light. Normally the rising sun fell over him in a yellow crawl, waking him slowly, but this morning's brightness had been flashed onto his face by a female pale ape. He blinked up, seeing dirty jeans, cream skin, inky hair. If not for the gratefulness he felt to her—the warmth they'd shared in the night had provided him with the best dreams he'd seen in decades—he would have jumped at her throat and spilt her life onto the water boardwalk. No creature can stare so insolently at the Esk God and believe they'll walk away unbleeding.

His mercy lasted long enough for her to escape. As he blinked again she lowered the boat that had sheltered them through the night, curtaining him again with darkness.

He felt her footsteps knocking away through the wood and considered going back to sleep, but without her hot stomach there would be no return to the dreams. Instead he flattened his furry torso, slithered out onto the dock and slipped into his river, where the fading visions were washed clean out of him. In his freshwater kingdom he had no need to dwell on such dry thoughts—he had streams, rivers, lakes to fly through, endless tributaries that parted before his webbed toes and waterproof fur, and everything in it knew who was in charge, who their god was, who would live and rule and smite until the river itself was drained to dust.

The thronging eels cleared out of his way, bending their backs and hissing their fealty, as he kicked under the twin bridges that hung over the mouth of his South Esk. Rakali, water rat, pest—the names meant nothing to him. He had been here longer than the loud pale apes, longer even than the quieter dark ones who had arrived earlier. He had seen them grow and die and spread, and he knew them far better than they would ever know themselves. With his blunt nose he could smell their foul industries; with the blanched tip of his tail he could feel their intrusions in the water; with his black eyes he could see the iron they sunk into his rivers, building dams, dropping anchors, hooking fish. He had learned the colour and the shape of their callousness, but he could not stop them, for his power was limited to the rivers, while they swamped over everything.

In summer, here in the mouth of his river, juvenile apes in fluorescent costumes would be plunging into the water around him, hurling themselves from rocky ledges. But in this early touch of winter they would not venture into his domain—another thing he knew about them. Their hairless skin would pop and shiver, and what puny strength they had would be shaken from their wobbling limbs. He knew they only swam in the heat, that they spat out saltwater, that they feared the deeper currents and did not know how to navigate them. And he knew that some of them were different; that some grew horns from their temples (horns their fellow apes could not see), some cried tree sap, some licked lips with bladed tongues and some, like the warm-stomached girl, returned after their ash had been scattered into the winds. He even knew why it happened—or at least he thought he did, and to a god thinking is the same as knowing.

He paddled upwards, feeling the current flow over his fur without ever impeding his progress. Soon he was snaking into a great basin that lay in the heart of a high-cliffed gorge. Out in the centre of the water he rolled over, turned his dark back fur to the chalky depths, showing his golden underbelly to the brightening sky. As his body warmed up, a heat that began on his navel and spread out to his extremities, he was reminded of the warm-stomached girl. It pleased him to remember that he had allowed her to live; something about the blaze in her gut told him she needed to be out there, that there was a purpose to her heat, that her blood belonged in her body and not in his mouth. He was accustomed to these instincts and knew them to be trustworthy, because to the Esk God they weren't instincts at all—they were facts.

Plus: he knew her father. And as powerful as the Esk God was, he didn't want to pick a fight with him.

A chairlift crawled along an iron rope high above him. Its shadow sprayed over his belly, momentarily shielding the sun's warmth, which was enough to get him moving again. He flipped over and headed upriver, swimming onwards towards the mountain that the dark apes called turbunna and the pale apes called Ben Lomond. The source of his rivers, the source of his world, the home of his high-living love: the Cloud God.

She was his creator, his meaning, his life. At her whim the clouds wrung water onto the lichen-scarred dolerite of the mountain, water that ran and dripped down into funnelling tongues that grooved into his rivers. Without the Cloud God there would be no Esk rivers, and without the rivers there would be no Esk God. As a result, his love for her was not a love of choice; he loved her infallibly. He went to see her at the rise of every new moon, and the only reason for these visits was love—he could not talk to her; he could not ask anything of her; he could not influence her in any way. He had never even seen her. He had only witnessed the flowing hem of her dress and the misty shape of her ankles as she wandered through the fog up on the heights of Stacks Bluff. As he shivered on the tall rocks, far from anywhere a rakali should ever go, he would imagine what she looked like. He imagined the Cloud God as a wedge-tailed eagle, as a powdery moth, as a floating albatross. And once he left the heights to attend to his river he kept imagining these things,

41

kept wondering what shape his love took.

He imagined on as he kept swimming upriver, until he reached a series of knife-sharp rapids. Here the water was cut up and foamy and dangerous, but not to a rakali, and especially not to the Esk God. He breezed up the rocks, morphing, shimmying, kicking and flying, turning waves into ladders and hard rocks into coiled springs. Soon he reached the grey wall of the Trevallyn Dam, which halted all other up-swimmers; but not him. His diamond claws sunk into the cement wall like it was made of wet clay and he surged upwards, gravity no more an impediment than the currents and rapids, and then he was over the wall and into the placid, hateful dam.

Here he did not stay long. This faux-lake led him to anger, and the river, no matter how damaged, did not need an angry god, for what good would it do for him to take his rage out on his subjects and dominion? What would change if he were to rip down jetties, chew through drainpipes, massacre the Labradors that drank from his shores? He was wise enough to know that his fury would not help the river or stop the apes, so he continued on, soothing his rage in a simple, humble way—by nipping screws out of the hull of an idle jetski.

Out of the dam and through the unsculpted banks he went, and how glorious it felt to snake his way into the green-brown embrace of his true river! How softly his water held him, how gently the reeds caressed him! His journey slowed into a lazy float, and as he bobbed past the waterfront mansions he forgot about the hateful dam. The land around his river let go of the suburbs and flattened into blond fields. The Esk God poked a pink tongue into the water and tasted run-off, lime, nitrogen and many other elements he could notice but not influence. South past the town of Hadspen he went, where he dived underwater to snap the neck of an ape-introduced trout (something he did as often as he could), and then on past more fields, more rusting iron tractors, past Longford, past Perth, past Evandale, and on and on southeast towards the unseen Cloud God. And maybe he would see her, this day; maybe he would finally catch a glimpse of her face.

The grass on the banks he passed shone brown-blond in the light, but where tree and fence shadows fell there were still broad white patches of frozen dew, courtesy of the Frost God, with whom the Esk God feuded over ice thickness every winter. Every now and then he hunted for yabbies underneath the workings of the Shale God. The Gum God's nuts rolled into the water from every direction, the Fur God's minions thumped beats through the soil that reverberated into the water's flesh, and the Bark God's cast-off hides fell from their trunks and floated along the surface of his river. And in all of these workings the Esk God noticed how diminished their presence was; how in years past everything in the land and water had consisted of a wider grandness; how the blood-tasting tang of iron had filtered into all that he saw and smelt and touched.

As he cruised around a willow-strangled bend his attention was snagged by a flick of colour in the sky. He rolled

over to see the curved yellow beak, red eyes and snow
plumage of a goshawk descending towards him, great talon
extended. Another rakali would be staring up at sharp death
but the Esk God merely lifted his tail from the water, it
white tip mirroring the white feathers of the falling bird
Seconds before impact the goshawk saw this white tail;
saw the too-gold colour of its prey's belly; it saw the black
humour in the blacker eyes; and then it was pulling out of its
dive, turning from bulleting doom into an awkward, wide
flapping mess of panic. If it had made contact it would have
had to answer to its own master (the Wing God or the Hunt
God: the Esk God couldn't remember)—that is, if the Esk
God had let it live after such a transgression. Now it regained
its skyward composure and soared away, far and fast, and the
Esk God laughed bubbles into his whiskers before remembering that it was the Wing God who the goshawk would be
reckoning with, because the Hunt God was dead—harried
tortured and finally killed by the pale apes, its doglike face
and black stripes forever gone.

But the Esk God remained, and the Esk God thrived
for who could kill a river? Now, near the farms of Avoca, his
domain skirted the edge of a eucalypt forest, where he paused
sniffed and climbed out to sit on a protruding taproot. He
was closing in on his destination—at his current speed he
would arrive at the South Esk's source inside an hour, and
there was no need to rush. The Cloud God would be waiting
for him, high on the peaks and plateaus where she poured her
sky water down the slopes and into his rivery veins.

He should have eaten by now—not that he needed to eat, but he should, because central to his duties was keeping life in the river in balance. He was about to dive back into the water when he saw something move on the opposite bank: a yabby, sitting on a pile of reeds, just where the water bumped against the soil. The Esk God was onto it in seconds, his fast feet latching onto the soft shell as his teeth nipped into its head. The yabby's claws flailed up at him but he was too fast, too strong, and besides, the yabby had no choice—its deity had issued a decree.

As he feasted the Esk God felt something lurch beneath him. The soil was moving. He dropped the dead yabby to look around, and saw that he was in the air, standing now on an iron grate that had been submerged in the mud. Iron fences loomed on either side of him, above him hung an iron roof, and carrying the iron contraption was the fleshy hand of a male pale ape. Two brown eyes descended to stare into the trap, and a moronic yellow-toothed smile appeared on the ape's face. It made a gurgling, floppy noise and hoisted the god into the air.

A deep hiss began forming in the Esk God's throat. His first instinct was to rip this flimsy cage to pieces and eviscerate the wobbling flesh of his captor, but he was paused by the smugness of the ape's smile. No, the Esk God thought. He would wait until this fool had opened the door of the trap and then he would leap out, a whir of gold-black death, and he would feel the smile morph into agony as the ape's muscles melted under his fangs.

The ape turned the cage vertical and opened it from above. The Esk God tensed; he just needed to wait for th face to come closer. A gloved hand descended into his priso and gripped its fumbly fingers around his body. Now the Es God leaned back on his tendons and sprang, releasing the fu and dreadful force of his wrath, but—nothing. He remaine wrapped in ape-grip. He sprang again, and again he did no move. Now he was being lifted from the trap, against hi will. How was his invincible might not snapping the twigg bones in this creature's hand? What foul sorcery was this Now he was close to the hated face, so close he could fee its foul breath staining his whiskers as the ape turned hir over, inspecting every inch of his glorious body with grubb eyes. The ape muttered something, and though the Esk Go could detect the tone of wonder and appreciation in the voic he could not understand the words, and he did not want to either. He wanted to escape and smite and murder. He wrig gled and twisted against the caging fingers, eliciting a laug from his captor, and his rage grew so monstrous he made vow to himself: once he had shredded this ape into worn meat he would go after every one of his tribe. He woul drown them in the gorges. He would open their throats an fling them off their bridges. He would fill his rivers wit their bloated bodies.

The ape had pulled a grey blade from his belt and wa holding it above the Esk God's neck. A quick aim; a har thrust; and suddenly the knife had pierced his immorta hide, and tapped into his vital blood. The Esk God learn

46

the feeling of iron against muscle. A bright feeling. A cold feeling. He squeaked in pain (a god squeaking!) and through the agony he still didn't understand what was happening. The blade sawed deeper, and as the strength ebbed out of his limbs the Esk God himself ebbed, in throbbing tides, out of his body. He began floating upwards, not on the current of a river but on the current of a thermal updraft. The Esk God rose, looking down at the ape clutching his body, and as he went higher, as he passed the floury curl of a cloud, his divine rage was shoved aside by a stupendous realisation: he was going to see her. Up here, released from his flesh, he would at last meet the Cloud God.

Up he rose, blue sky and patchwork earth masked more and more by the clouds. She was close; she had never been closer; and in the final moments before he saw her face he remembered the dream he'd had the night before, the dream ushered into his mind by the heat of the warm-stomached girl. He'd been lying on the grassy bank of the great gorge basin near the mouth of his South Esk. A hot sun was warming his belly. He became so warm that he rolled over to heat his back, and then, staring outwards, he saw what this intense heat had done to the water: the far side of the basin was hidden by a towering wall of flames. These flames were spreading across the cliffs and trees of the gorge; ghost-blue flames, playing on the water, licking all they touched into a dance of crumbling ash; and his river had never been more glorious.

# FUR

Mr Hough,

Please forgive me for contacting you out of the blue. I was given this address by your editor—as you have no website, phone number or email address, she was kind enough to pass it on after I called your publisher's office.

First, I want to say how much I admire your book. *The Wooden Jacket* has been an extremely helpful reference in an endeavour I am currently undertaking. It is this endeavour that has led me to seek you out.

I need a coffin for my sister. I make no exaggeration when I say that it must be perfect. She will be the first woman in our family to be buried (traditionally they have been cremated), and I will spare no expense in making sure that her final resting place fits her as comfortably as her own skin.

I am convinced that you are the only man who will truly understand what I mean and what I require. If you are able to provide me with any assistance, I will happily pay you.

Yours sincerely,
Levi McAllister

Mr Idiot,

You scum. You ill-mothered baboon. You parasitic swine-herding subhuman mongoloid. What has made you believe it appropriate to hound me through the postal service, simply because I am the author of an (admittedly classic) piece of coffee-table literature? How dare you pursue me in such an underhanded fashion! I have built myself a quiet life of monastic contemplation in a place of rare beauty (which you well know, seeing as you have discovered my address) and all I ask of the world is that it leaves me alone. Yet here the world is, and you are its agent, fracturing my peace with your frivolous drivel. I am inclined to visit you myself and teach you a lesson in etiquette with the hairy side of my learned hand.

As for your request: I do not undertake work for unsolicited clients. You mentioned remuneration, but I doubt you will be able to afford my fees—due to my unparalleled expertise in this field, my rates are very high. Judging from the quality of your manners and handwriting I assume you didn't finish your schooling, and it is my experience that a lack of education generally leads to a penniless life. Do not contact me again.

Thurston Hough

Mr Hough,

I apologise for offending you with my previous letter.
I realise how rude it was, and I am genuinely sorry for
upsetting your peace. Under normal circumstances I would
never have done it—but I am desperate. I hate to blurt out
personal details, but my mother recently died and my sister
is struggling to cope with the loss. She is barely clinging to
the edge of her sanity and I believe this is due to fears about
her own death. For reasons I'd rather not go into, securing
her a suitable coffin may put some of these fears to rest. It
may be a long shot, but I must do something. I cannot allow
her pain to continue.

With regard to your fees: I am willing to pay you up to
$5,000 for your advice on this matter. I am also able to pay a
larger amount of money if you are in a position to offer help
beyond basic tips.

Yours sincerely,
Levi McAllister

Mr Moron,

Congratulations, cretin. You have ignited within me a fury so incandescent it rivals the heat and destructive capability of the sun. I instructed you not to contact me again, yet here I find myself RESPONDING TO ANOTHER ONE OF YOUR MORONIC MISSIVES!

However, you are in luck, thanks to your frankly astounding reserves of capital. Who did you rob? If I discover that this money is ill-gained I will not hesitate to inform the authorities.

But I digress: the joyful thought of you rotting in a dark cell distracted me from the matter at hand. The reason I am reluctantly willing to aid you is because—through no fault of my own—I am currently in a precarious financial position, due to a longstanding difference of opinion with the Tax Department. Scoundrels and thieves, the lot of them. I have been evading their clutches for years, but my evil neighbours—whose ranks are led by a nosy, disgustingly promiscuous old crone named Mavis, who is a prominent member of the local Country Women's Association (which, I assume you are aware, is actually a terrorist group)—must have alerted them to my whereabouts. So please understand: I care not one jot for the emotions of your mission or for your weepy wuss of a sister. I am purely in need of capital to stave off the malicious malingering of these government bandits.

And your luck extends (as long as your wallet does), for I am more than simply an expert in this field; I have also applied this expertise to the physical craft of building coffins. My hands are as talented as my mind, and my instinct for beauty matches my eye for detail. My woodworking skills have grown to a point that I can confidently claim to be not only the world's foremost expert in all things sarcophagi; I am also the world's finest coffin maker.

So—as well as furnishing your feeble mind with knowledge that no other man on earth possesses, for an appropriate fee I can also craft your sister's final vessel with my own hands. Rest assured that I will only use the finest timber to create this coffin (provided you can afford the cost of the materials), as well as a precious fur inlay to provide her with uncommon comfort as she passes into the next life. I use high-grade wombat pelts sourced from a premium supplier in the far south, ensuring all my coffins are more luxurious than a royal featherbed.

If you wish to proceed with this course of action you must decide swiftly. I am a very busy man and do not have the time nor the patience to accommodate any dilly-dallying. Nor do I wish to engage in a drawn-out exchange of correspondence. If you are willing to engage my services, please respond by sending me your sister's age, measurements and probable cause of death, i.e. what she is dying from.

Thurston Hough

Mr Hough,

Thank you for your response. I would indeed like to hire you to build my sister's coffin. For this service I am capable of paying you a further $22,000 on top of the initial $5,000 I offered for your advice. I trust this will cover the cost of the materials as well as your fees.

Charlotte is twenty-three. I have attached her measurements to the back of this letter. As for her condition, I must not have made myself clear in my previous letters—for this I apologise. She is not suffering from any illnesses or diseases, nor does she have any pre-existing conditions or tendencies that are of any immediate concern to her well-being. Other than her mental frailties, she is currently in a state of good health (although I haven't seen her for a few days). I don't need this coffin to bury her in; I need it as physical proof that she won't be cremated. She will eventually be laid to rest in it, of course, but not for many, many years. I hope this unusual circumstance doesn't upset your process.

Yours sincerely,
Levi McAllister

Mr Nincompoop,

Mr Hough,

I regret to inform you that you have been addressing your letters to an incorrect address. This is not the office of the Guinness World Records, where you are clearly trying to set the record for buffoonery and incompetence. This is the home of a scholar and craftsman who has no time for your brain-shattering levels of stupidity!

My process, which you claim to have been mindful of, depends <u>entirely</u> on the condition of the subject at the time of their death. From reading *The Wooden Jacket* (if you weren't lying; I am starting to doubt whether you can read at all) you should know that different varieties of timber have wildly different reactions when they are filled with corpses and interred into the earth. For example, a coffin made with blackwood panels will ensure that no trees can grow within a fifty-metre radius of the plot where it has been buried—no trees, that is, other than the single blackwood that sprouts directly from the coffin's heart. This tree will grow far larger than an ordinary specimen, towering above the barren landscape. And in almost all cases it will host a tenant: a single black-faced cormorant (a bird usually found clinging to coastal rocks) will create a nest in its highest branches, endlessly peeling off a loud, soul-rending cry into the sky. If anyone wanders too close to the blackwood the cormorant will swoop down and deliver bloody justice to the unlucky invader.

Golden wattle, on the other hand, that capricious, fluffy-dusty do-gooder of a plant, will produce an entirely different result. A coffin built from wattle will initially have no discernible affect, but after a week the air around the plot begins to take on an unmistakable odour. This smell has variously been described as that of a never-cleaned public toilet, a mountain of fish guts, the rotting gums of a lifelong liquorice fanatic, and a bonfire of pubic hair. All accounts say it is the worst smell the author has ever encountered.

Or take native myrtle. Any plant that sprouts from the soil surrounding a myrtle coffin will begin producing large red berries. Weeds, trees, hedges, even flowers—all will burst forth with orbs of scarlet fruit. Taut-skinned and tumescent, they are not poisonous, but they do taste strongly of copper. Anyone who eats this fruit will develop an intense desire for red meat, particularly beef carpaccio and black pudding. On some occasions this hunger has driven these fruit-eaters to devour any meat raw, or even—if urban myths are to be believed—to gnaw on the limbs of strangers, loved ones or themselves.

And there are more, many more—you have my book; I need not go on. So you should realise, idiot though you are, that I must have some sort of sense of the person I am putting in the ground. It would be erroneous to bury someone who was popular and gregarious in life in a box of blackwood—a solitary tree that houses a territorial seabird would be an inappropriate ending for their physical remains (and make it very hard for their friends and family to pay their respects). It would, however, be seemly to put an axe murderer in a myrtle coffin, to create within the landscape a permanent reminder of their bloody crime.

I should decline this work and discontinue our correspondence. However, other events have forced my hand. Yesterday I received a pink-bordered letter from the Tax Department that featured such words as 'overdue', 'bankruptcy' and 'collection agency'. How dare these tax cretins hound me! How dare a moron like Mavis and her fanatical, hate-mongering Country Women's Association set them on my trail! Rather than waging war with these devils (and I could, you know; I am a crack shot with an air rifle) I have decided to push ahead with your project, despite the challenges your ignorance presents. The amount you mentioned in your previous letter will be enough to get these leeches off my back, at least for a while.

And before your underdeveloped mind starts fretting about what sort of coffin I'm building, do not fear. I have long found that the most appropriate material for those who have died young is wood taken from the many-hued whorls of an old snowgum. Its hard, cold-to-the-touch timber does not rot or warp or even fade. Instead it fossilises, and so too does the body it contains. The flesh of the dead turns as hard and unyielding as the stony coffin, and cannot be altered by any natural means. This way the beauty of the young—I assume your sister is beautiful; what twenty-three-year-old woman is not?—is preserved for all time. I understand she isn't dying right now, but she could die at any time, so snowgum is undoubtedly the safest and smartest option.

I should also mention that I won't be using wombat fur as inlay. I know I claimed that this is my usual practice, but it seems my suppliers in the south are suffering from some farming difficulties. To address this fur shortage I have taken to trapping water rats. They are plentiful in the South Esk River, which flows past my homestead, and their fur is perhaps even softer and thicker than that produced by wombats. In fact, only a few days ago I trapped an unusually large specimen with the finest coat I have ever seen. Mottled black on top, with a glowing golden belly, it is always warm to the touch, even when laid outside under a winter moon. I find myself running my fingers through it whenever I am working. It is truly a wondrous pelt, and will be the perfect furnishing for your sister's last resting place.

Now I am off to scale the heights of Ben Lomond to select a snowgum to harvest, saw and shape into a coffin. Do not bother me with any more of your inane enquiries. Rest assured that work has begun.

Thurston Hough

Mr Hough,

Thank you. Snowgum sounds like a fantastic choice.
I'm sure that Charlotte will agree, once she sees the result.

In the meantime, please let me know if there is anything
I can do to assist you.

Yours sincerely,
Levi McAllister

Mr Hough,

I have not heard from you in a fortnight. I trust that work on my sister's coffin is going well. I wanted very much to tell her about our project, but she has still not returned home. Don't worry—there have been reports of her travelling through various towns, and as I write the police are looking for her. I'm sure this is just a part of her grieving process.

Also, I have a lot of free time at the moment. Do you require any assistance with the construction of her coffin? I don't mean to imply that you might need it—I am simply offering help in the form of manual labour.

Yours sincerely,
Levi McAllister

Mr Faecal Brain,

Mr Hough,

For the love of all that is precious and beautiful in the world, leave me alone! I do not care about the shameless wanderings of your strumpet sister, nor do I want you anywhere near my workshop. The work is progressing at a normal rate. Building the finest coffins in the world takes time.

There is only one thing you can do for me: poison the South Esk River. For some unholy reason the denizens of this accursed stream have taken to harassing me whenever I go to the water's edge. Water rats, eels, blackfish, herons, frogs, even the occasional platypus—they are all trying to kill me! The horrid creatures bite at my toes and legs every chance they get. The birds even take wing at the sight of me and try to winkle my eyes out with their dagger-like beaks. I am under siege, McAllister, from the moment I stray within twenty metres of the river. The world has gone mad. Tax pirates, letter writers, killer river beasts: they are all out to end me. Such is the price of genius, I suppose.

But do not worry. I am getting on with the construction of the coffin. The snowgum I harvested from the cliffs of the mountain has yielded a fine grain of wood, and its planks are strong and straight. Coupled with the glorious water-rat pelt, it could be my greatest work yet. I should be finished within the month. Unless you can kill everything in the river, I beg of you: leave me alone.

Thurston Hough

Mr Hough,

It's been a month since you last wrote to me. Can you please provide me with an update on your progress? I'm sorry to hear about your troubles with the South Esk. I too have been experiencing some difficulties—the police were unable to find my sister. They say that they're still searching for her, but one officer told me privately that they believe she's moved interstate and they aren't putting many resources into the case. I've resorted to hiring a private detective.

Yours sincerely,
Levi McAllister

Mr Quivering Pile of Irritation Made Human,

This is the last time you will hear from me. Not just because the experience of reading all these pointless stories about your gypsy sister has been more unpleasant than seeing my dentist and proctologist in the same afternoon; our communication must cease because I am unable to complete the coffin you commissioned.

I have never before reneged upon a deal. Nor am I the sort of person who makes excuses. I will simply give you the facts: I am besieged in my own home by the creatures of the river. The last time I wrote to you they were only molesting me when I ventured near their accursed waterway—now they are actively harassing me whenever I poke a foot out my front door. Yabbies tap their claws against my windows, glaring in at me with their demented bug-eyes. Herons circle above my property like vultures on the plain. Eels squirm across my lawn to bite at my feet, dying in packs on the grass. Drakes assault my outer walls with their horrid beaks and corkscrew genitalia. But the worst, the most persistent, the most hateful are the water rats. They have started digging at the foundations of my house like dogs at a beach. During daylight hours I shoot at them from the window, but at night they return, always in greater quantities than before, scratching and nibbling and scouring away at the wood and dirt my house is built upon. In the darkness I peer out and see the devilish lights of their eyes, surrounding me as they scurry about, enacting their hell-driven mischief. I am sure that their number has climbed into the hundreds. And if I cannot find a way to stop them, I am equally sure that my number is up.

Your coffin lies half-finished in my workshop. As odious as the thought of actually meeting you in person is, you are welcome to come and collect it in its current state, and attempt to complete it yourself. But you shall not be taking the glorious water rat pelt with you; it has become my sole comfort in these troubling times. I spend hours at my front window with my fingers immersed in the endless warmth of its fur, while my other hand grips my trusty rifle. At night I lay it over my pillowcase, where it heats my cheek throughout all of my fitful dreams. Even to gaze upon its wondrous lustre lifts my spirits. It is dear to me in ways I cannot hope to describe.

So come: collect your half-made coffin. I shall not charge you for it, even though I have laboured over its creation. I no longer need the money—the taxman has no chance of getting to me while these creatures plague my doorstep. Come take the flesh-stoning panels of freshly carved snowgum. But the pelt stays with me, moron boy. The only grave it shall adorn is my own.

Thurston Hough

# ICE

You shouldn't drink gin before you drive a sedan. But you also shouldn't talk back to your mother, wear black with blue or sleep with loose men, and I'd done all those things plenty of times, so I didn't hesitate when I soaked my throat with a thick finger of Tanqueray before I hit the road.

New client. Weird kid—or at least he'd seemed weird on the phone. Tweaky voice, even though his words were smooth. Like his private-school manners were paved over something that had cracked. Even before I met him I didn't trust him. But I needed the cash, and I needed the work—too much time between cases let a muddy fog waft into my thoughts. It was better to stay busy.

He lived on a farm on the coast between Beauty Point

and Hawley Beach, about an hour's drive from my flat in north Launceston. I burned up the East Tamar Highway, tyres sliding across the black ice that filmed over the road on every shadowed corner. I shouldn't drive so fast. The Lancer can't handle it. It's handled a lot of things, but black ice: it's never been able to come to terms with that. The third time I spun out I grudgingly slowed down, crawling all the way to the Batman Bridge, where the light sprayed over the broad blue river, forcing me to blink and grunt and yank down the visor. It sure was pretty, all that light on all that water. I'm not interested in pretty things.

I made it to the farm twenty minutes later, although it wasn't really a farm, or not what I thought a farm should be. There were no sheep. No cows. No pigs or geese or goats. No barking dogs, shearing sheds or irrigation machines. There was just a lonely dirt road, a sandstone cottage and a few thistle-filled fields that sloped down to the grey ocean. How this kid made money had me beat. But as long as he had it, I didn't care.

I parked next to the cottage and knocked on the door, which he opened a few moments later. In the dim light I couldn't make him out that well, but when he invited me inside I got a proper look. Skinny face. Skinny arms. Skinny everything. He offered me tea. I declined, but he boiled the jug anyway, said he needed a pick-me-up, sounding nervous and shaky. As the water heated he had a go at a bit of chit-chat—how he'd seen my ad in the paper, how he'd assumed I was a man, whether the drive was all right; all the usual small talk that I don't go in for.

Eventually the jug clicked off, and then we were sitting at the table in his little kitchen, me picking at my cuticles, him sipping and telling me what I could do for him. The story wasn't as unusual as he thought it was. Mother dies, daughter goes bonkers, son acts like nothing's wrong, daughter runs away. He could've told me this in an email. Sure, the whole reincarnation thing was a bit off-script, but I'd seen stranger things happen to stranger people—blackmailers who'd stolen souls with high-powered cameras; thieves who'd sold their shadows to puppeteers; adulterers who'd swapped faces with gargoyles. You name it, I'd seen it. And I'd investigated it, solved it, and been home by nine with a glass of gin and a thick sandwich. Skinny boy's mother and all her twice-dead relatives didn't make me blink.

He handed me a photo of the sister as he spoke. Normal-looking girl in her early twenties. Dark hair, like his. Pale skin. A bit of mongrel in her face, I'd guess, but you never really know about that until you see someone fired up. I slipped it into my pocket. When he stopped talking I took out my notebook. *Did the cops find anything?*

He rubbed his face. *Not really. She was travelling south. The last place she was spotted was on a bus headed to Franklin. I went down there myself, but nobody had seen her.* He was trying to sound calm, but there was that nervous shake again, wobbling about beneath his tongue.

*Who was the lead on the case?*

*Pardon?*

*The lead. The detective.*

*Oh.* He frowned and got up to fetch his wallet from the kitchen bench, pulled out a blue card. *Senior Detective Graham Malik.* He looked back at me. *You know him?*

I tugged on a stubborn piece of skin. *Somewhat.* Graham Malik. The Last Graham. At least I'd be dealing with a face I knew. I stood up and smoothed back my hair.

*That's it?* He swung forward from the bench. *You don't need anything else?*

*Nah.* I grabbed my coat from the back of the chair and made for the door, where I paused. I'm a master of the doorway pause. *Except one thing.* Now I turned to see what his face would do when I asked: *Where's your old man's place?*

The cracks I'd heard in his voice swam up to his face, snapping over those pointy little cheekbones. *Why?*

*A girl goes missing, you generally check her dad's place first.*

*She's not there.*

*Probably not. But I'm still going to check.*

His voice rushed out, high and jittery. *That isn't necessary.*

I crossed my arms. *You want me to find her?*

*Of course.*

*Then let me do my job.*

He had a go at staring me down and lost, badly. With wet eyes he grabbed a letter from the bench and marched over, handing it to me. *Here.* It was addressed to a Jack McAllister at a property down the highway, closer to Launceston. I slipped the envelope into my pocket and made to leave, but the kid wasn't done talking. *When will I hear from you? I'd appreciate updates.*

I'd appreciate a long weekend with some Olympic gymnasts, I thought. But I didn't bother telling him. I just opened the door and felt the wind slap my face. *I'll be in touch.*

Δ

Half an hour later I arrived at the old man's house. It was a big timber pile just south of Exeter, perched on a bend overlooking the Tamar. The sun was falling fast, dropping behind the western hills, dragging shadows over the valley.

The house was something else. I don't go much for ostentatious architecture, but I could appreciate what was going on here. Three storeys, two chimneys, at least five bedrooms. Built out of some kind of rich red timber that almost glowed, but that might've been the dusky light. Myrtle, I guessed, although I don't know anything about wood. The mansion was surrounded by a sprawling, overgrown garden, flowers and bushes and all sorts of scrub pushing firmly against each other in what must have once, years ago, been a vast garden. Trees thrust up through the foliage, towering over the house, competing for the light. Some part of me realised that, like the view from the bridge, it was all rather pretty. I stopped looking at it.

No lights were shining from any of the windows, no smoke was pumping from either of the chimneys and no sound was coming from under any of the doors. No cars in the driveway, either. I knocked anyway, expecting nothing and getting it. No father to be found. I'd check with Malik in the morning. I jumped back in the Lancer, swung the wheel and headed back out onto the highway, but not before I'd seen something I'd missed on the way in: a broad, blackened patch of burnt grass in the lawn, right in front of the house. The grass around it had grown high and lush, but this ring of charcoal had not recovered. I thought of the mother, the one who'd burned twice, and felt a brief twinge.

By the time I'd followed the river home it was completely dark. I parked in the alley, let myself into the flat, and made a ham and mustard sandwich. A glass of gin happened too, and another few, until I was lying on the couch watching someone shout at me from the television. At some point the neighbour's cat came in, a huge black tom that had taken a liking to me. I couldn't tell how it kept getting in. It sat on my stomach as I fed it strips of ham. More gin. The room turned swimmy. I'd find the girl in the morning. As long as she hadn't become a ring of burnt grass.

Δ

In the morning my brain was having a fight with my skull and I hated pretty much everything, but that was normal. I shoved the tom off me and began my breakfast routine: toast, black coffee, push-ups, sit-ups, hot shower, toothbrush, Panadol, clothes. By the time I was pushing buttons through my shirt I was as good as I was going to get. In the mirror I saw that my hair was reaching past my ears. I smoothed it back, wiped on some cherry lipstick, sorted my eyes out with a bit of liner, grabbed my coat and got out of the flat before I had to look at it for any longer.

It wasn't far to the cop shop. All the nature strips I walked past were covered in a brittle layer of frost; the local footy oval was a glistening white pan. I remembered my playing days, and the feeling of my body crunching into the ice after an early start in the under-fourteens, my skin first going sharp, then numb, then stinging for hours until the match was over. I didn't miss it.

I kept walking, over the bridge and into town, my hangover coming too but having the decency to stay more or less quiet. On my way past a bakery I stepped in to buy a couple of croissants. The sugar in the air put a perk in my stride, and by the time I reached the station I was feeling almost fine. At the front desk a junior cop wanted to know if I had a complaint. I drew on a smile. *I'm here to see Senior Detective Malik.*

*What case would you like to speak to the senior detective about? He's very busy.* The boy-cop smiled back, and behind his too-white teeth I could see his fragile little thoughts tracing lines, making assumptions, bouncing off words like Duty and Career and Citizen and Safety.

*I'm his ex-wife. Tell him I'm on the way up.* I started moving towards a door in the rear left corner of the room, the one that led up to the detectives' desks. It didn't open for me, so I turned back to the officer. *Or I could just call my lawyer.* I pulled out my phone. *The number's on speed-dial. Graham would love that.*

He blinked, and his neon smile flickered away into the stale cop-shop air. My thumb hovered over the keypad. He blinked again and pressed a button underneath the desk. The door began slowly opening. I gave him a mock salute and started climbing the stairs.

Three flights up and I was banging on a glass door emblazoned with Malik's name and rank. *Come in—Jesus,* he barked, so I yanked on the handle and strode into the office of the Last Graham. A squat, lumpy boulder of a man was leaning over a chipped desk, shuffling through a stack of finely printed paper. His sleeves were rolled up past his hairy forearms, and even though the morning was freezing and the station had shithouse heating there were little circles of sweat rolling down his bare, coffee-brown scalp. *Look, Patricia, you've already got my balls. What the hell else do you...*

He looked up as I planted myself in the stiff guest chair. *Morning, Graham.*

*You son of a bitch.* He collapsed into his own seat and kicked ineffectively at the pile of paper. *I thought you were Patricia. She's taking me to the cleaners, you know.*

*I heard.* I tore open the bag of croissants and placed it on the desk between us.

*Fucking bitch. Kids, house, kayak, everything.*

I raised an eyebrow. *You kayak?*

He snatched up one of the croissants. *I did. When I had a fucking kayak.* The whole pastry disappeared into his mouth, golden crumbs spraying over the papers. *Anyway. What do you want?*

They called him the Last Graham for two reasons: first, because the name Graham had been so unpopular for newborn babies for the last few decades it was highly likely

72

that once a few old codgers kicked the bucket he, Graham Malik, would be the last Graham on the island. Second, because he was perceived to be so slow—physically and mentally—that he was always the last detective to solve anything. The first part was true. The second was up for discussion, but he was by no means as bad a cop as many people would have you think. Over the years he had given me tips that had helped me close more than a few cases I'd been struggling with. I don't know why. Maybe I reminded him of a long-lost little sister. Or maybe it was just the occasional froth of testosterone. Who knows why men do what they do? He'd also looked the other way when I'd twisted the odd arm, on more than one occasion. I trusted him, and more importantly I respected him, even when his colleagues didn't.

*The missing McAllister girl. Her brother's hired me to find her. Turns out he's not happy with your efforts.*

*Oh. That one.* He kept chewing. *The boys think she's done a runner. Big tragedy, dead mother and whatever, and she wants out of her life without being followed. Plus, she wants to get away from that creepy brother of hers.* He grabbed another croissant. *You know she was last seen on the bus to Franklin?* I nodded. *Gone down south to throw off the scent, the boys think, then snuck back up north and moved interstate. Once she's crossed Bass Strait we can't do much.*

*You don't think she's in trouble?*

*The boys don't.*

I leaned forward. *What about you?*

He stopped chewing and swallowed. *Trouble? Maybe*

*not. We spoke to a couple of lads who had a crack at her in Tunbridge—they were of the opinion that she could look after herself pretty well. But...*

*But?*

*Look.* He folded his arms. Flakes of pastry fell from his torso like golden snow. *If someone snatched her, we'd know by now. If she were dead, someone would've found the body. But if she wanted to hide...she could do it.*

*So you think she's holed up somewhere.*

He shrugged. *Maybe. Or maybe she's gone to the mainland, like the boys reckon. It would make sense.*

*Not everything makes sense.*

*Sure doesn't.*

He handed me a file marked 'McAllister'. I got up, thought about shaking his hand, but didn't. The Last Graham wasn't into formalities, and I didn't want to upset the ecosystem of our relationship, so I just gave him one of my mock salutes. *Thanks.*

*Thanks for breakfast.*

I headed for the door, ready to go, sick of the musty stink of cops and filing cabinets. But as my fingers wrapped around the handle something from last night flashed into my brain: the timber mansion, the overgrown garden, the circle of burnt grass. I turned back to Malik. *What about the father?*

He was brushing the crumbs off his chest, aiming for a cupped serviette, missing more than he was collecting. *I don't know much about the guy. Nobody does.* He tried to play the line soft, but I caught the edge in it.

*And?*

He stopped brushing. *Well…the wife's family, the McAllisters—they're one of the oldest families you'll find around these parts. Been here for generations. Bit like those tuna hunters up the coast. But this Jack fella—he turned up out of nowhere. Don't know when, exactly. Just kind of…appeared. Flush with cash, mind you. No family. One day he just pops up, out of the blue, engaged to Edith McAllister, saying he'd been travelling through the area and she'd given him a reason to stay. Seemed like a nice guy, so nobody cared.*

*But you did.*

Another shrug. *I was a junior cop back then. So wet behind the ears I needed a lifejacket. What would I know?*

I tried to get more out of his expression, but his face was unreadable. And I didn't have time to focus on the girl's dad, no matter how mysterious he was. Right now I needed to follow the trail, and the trail led south. I pushed on the handle, but before I left I performed my patented door pause. *Good luck with Patricia.*

He aimed another kick at the pile of papers. *I don't need luck. I need a decent lawyer.* He swung his foot, missing everything. *Or maybe you could go talk to her. You know, you're a woman…*

*Your powers of deduction continue to astonish me.*

*You know what I mean. You could make her see reason.*

I looked out his dirty window. The sky was fat with grey clouds.

*Try flowers.*

Unlike a lot of people on this strange southern rock, I have no hidden talents. No magic tricks, no secret skills, no unnatural knack for anything. But if I had to admit to some kind of enhanced ability, I would tell you about my twinge. It's not a knee twinge, or a gut twinge, or even a twinge in the neck: it's a full-body, skin-shaking twinge that snaps right through me, from my heels to my hair, whenever something is about to go wrong. It's pretty accurate. I twinge when a thug is about to get violent, when a client is lying, when a trail goes dead. I even twinge before my tyres start to slip on black ice. It's a twinge I can trust, and I usually listen to it. I've got nothing else to rely on.

When the Last Graham told me about Jack McAllister, I twinged. I twinged so hard I thought I was going to fall through the window. But for the first time, nothing happened. No accident, no violence, nothing negative whatsoever. Graham kept talking, and I kept listening. There was a possibility it was a delayed twinge—triggered by the mention of something, foretelling a threat that was not yet obvious. That had never happened before, so I dismissed it. I convinced myself it was a rare misfire. Nothing to worry about.

We all make mistakes.

Δ

The Midlands Highway: the sort of road you'd call a goat track, if you had something against goat tracks. Lazy drivers wiped themselves out on the narrow lanes and shoulderless corners every second week, but no one ever slowed down. People don't learn; they just accumulate facts. I leaned on the accelerator as the Lancer and I bulleted over potholes, slowing down only on a gap-toothed bridge as we flew over the cold wet streak of the South Esk.

My first stop would be Tunbridge, where I knew Charlotte McAllister had had an altercation with a couple of gentlemen. The world whipped past me in an agricultural blur. Sheep clouded the fields. The sky kept thinking about rain without ever making a commitment to it. Bored by the ceaseless farmland I leaned my foot harder, and an hour later I hit Tunbridge.

Small town. A historic place, I'd been told once, but historic is just a dusty version of boring. Even worse than boring, it was pretty—sandstone houses, sun-dappled river-banks, flocks of waddling ducks, the whole shebang. I hated the place as soon as I saw it, but I'm not one to let a little bit of hatred get in the way of a pay cheque. It was mid-afternoon. I figured the two Romeos I was after would still be at work, so I parked by the bridge and staked out the front of the only pub in town.

At five or so the local farmhands, shop owners and old codgers started dribbling along the streets and through the pub doors. None of them looked like my marks, until I spotted two men in yellow high-vis jackets getting out of a paint-chipped ute. They matched the description in Charlotte's file—one was dark, languid and had his mouth shut, while the other was yammering away with a loose jaw as a fuzzy orange caterpillar crawled across his upper lip. They marched into the pub. I gave them enough time to say hello, order a drink, do whatever it is small-town men do when they walk into a bar, then followed them in.

I copped a few stares when I pushed through the doors. A thirty-something woman with hard eyes, dark lips and short hair isn't a common sight in the country. The men in high-vis were propped on the far side of the bar, so I ordered a straight gin and sunk into a split-leather booth, making sure we could see each other. They were cradling pints of lager and chatting up a storm—at least, the moustache was. The smoky one just sat, smiled and nodded. I could've gone over, shown them my photo of the McAllister girl and tried to sweet-talk the information out of them, but my gut told me they wouldn't give me anything. The boorish looks on their faces told me something else. I didn't like it, but I knew I could handle it. My gin went down sharp, and the barman soon got the idea that he could keep bringing it to me without having to fuss about with orders.

After an hour or so the locals began creaking out. The moustache was doing a bad job of staring at me out of the corner of his eye. I threw him a wink. It nearly knocked him off his stool. He muttered to his friend, who almost raised his eyebrows. The moustache kept wobbling out words, and then the two of them had pushed back their stools and were wandering towards me, full of cautious, half-drunk confidence.

*Evening*, said the moustache. I stared up at him for a moment, then indicated the other side of the booth with a tilt of my head. A velvet glow spread across his face and he slid onto the bench, followed by his partner.

*Havin' a good night?* The guy had something against silence. I liked him about as much as I liked tonic in my gin, but he was playing into my hands. I stared straight into his face, pulled a curl onto the corner of my mouth, and said: *Better now.*

And from there it was easy, so easy—why couldn't these underlaid bozos have given me at least the imitation of a challenge? Sweat slicked over Moustache's face and a hooded smile spread across Smoky's as I sipped, squirmed and suggested my way through the next few hours. I let Moustache do most of the talking—endless inane stories about the mines they'd worked in, the cars they'd owned, the friends they'd made and lost, the comparable qualities of coal, ore, copper, tin. He even, after his fourth or fifth beer, began telling me about their fathers, which was as close as I came to dropping my act and bailing on the case. Who wants to hear a grown man blabber on about his relationship with his father? But I kept a straight face, and when Smoky began rubbing a work boot along the inside of my ankle under the table I bit my lip at him and let him keep doing it.

When I had to speak, I told them I was an HR consultant who specialised in the field of change management, travelling from the capital to Launceston for work. All Moustache could say to that was *Sounds like a pretty full-on sort of job*, to which I replied, with something like a sultry sigh: *Exhausting.*

I'm no oil painting. Plenty of men have found plenty of ways to resist my advances. But in a certain mood and a certain light I do have an appeal—a flinty, slightly androgynous, I-wonder-if-I-could-handle-her sort of allure. And it helps that I've kept my face unscarred and my body in good nick. Anyway, what I had going on was clearly working on these chumps, so when I suggested that we go for a walk to appreciate the famous Tunbridge night air they were swaying towards the door faster than they could finish their beers.

Outside, I steered the three of us in the direction of the river. Moustache was on my left, brushing my arm with his own, while Smoky was on my right, letting his hand cup my thigh. I pulled a bottle of gin from my inner coat pocket and passed it round. They took long swigs and pretended it didn't burn. We reached the river and I sat down, beckoning them onto the grassy bank either side of me.

*So*, I said, taking another pull as they hunched close, *you guys do this often?*

Smoky was trailing a finger through a tuft behind my ear. Moustache answered. *Do what?*

*Show a girl from out of town a good time.*

*Well, we're always welcoming to visitors*, said Moustache, *aren't we?* He threw the question at his friend, but was ignored; Smoky was nuzzling at my neck.

*And other girls don't mind?* I bent into the spiky stubble. Moustache leaned closer.

*Mind what?*

*The two of you. At once.*

Now he started rubbing his hand up and down my thigh. *Sometimes. But we're always, you know.* His voice fell to a mumble. *Gentlemen.*

I had to play the next bit carefully; they were coming on too fast, and I needed to get more out of them. I kinked my neck away from Smoky and leaned back on my hands, putting a bit of distance between us all. *Of course. I mean, I don't mind at all. I like it.* Another slow drag of gin. *But some girls must've had...reservations.*

Moustache frowned; I'd pushed too far. But I stroked a finger down his chin and handed him the bottle, and after he took a sip he said: *There was one girl. The other week. We thought she was dead keen, wouldn't leave us alone. Then, just before, y'know...she flipped.* He waved a hand at the river. *Went mental.* He looked at Smoky. *Show her what she did.*

Smoky, who had lain down on the bank beside me, reached into his pocket and pulled out his phone. He turned on the screen and held it over his wrist, using the blueish glow to show me the large, silvery mark of a burn. I peered at it. *How'd she do that? With a lighter?*

Moustache answered for him. *No idea. She didn't have a lighter—well, I didn't see one. One second it's all good, next she's goin' nuts and kickin' the shit out of us and burning Davo. Fuckin' psycho.* Bitterness had crept into his voice. I kept stroking his chin, letting my fingers roll down to his collarbone.

*She from around here?*

He turned back to me. *Nah. She was goin' south. Kept*

*asking us about this mine we used to work at.*

Just a bit more. I only needed one more word from them. *Which mine?*

My luck, fickle at the best of times, held. *The tin one. At Melaleuca.* Moustache lay down on my left, as Smoky wriggled closer on my right. *We didn't tell her it's been closed for years. Only thing there now is a wombat farm.*

I put a hand behind his skull and pulled him close, whispering in his ear. *What a bitch.* I dropped my voice. *What a little slut.*

His breath pumped, fast and hot on my cheek. *Yeah,* he muttered, *she was a dumb fucken slut. Wasn't she, Davo?*

For the first and last time, I heard Smoky speak. *Total whore.*

I let them come to me, rubbing hands over my body, my shirt, my tits, my groin, lips whacking at my skin, tongues worming at my ears and mouth. I looked up at the pointy lights of the stars, blocking it all out, as I asked them both: *And what do you do to sluts?*

Smoky didn't answer, but Moustache's excitement intensified. He lifted his head, thinking of something to say, something from a porno or the slimy bin of his imagination, but for the first time that night he was lost for words. It didn't matter. While he was rummaging around for dirty talk he didn't see my fist clench and slam up into his jeans, although he certainly felt it, as surely as I felt a testicle squash between two of my knuckles. He gasped, hot wind and pain, and Smoky looked up in time to see my right elbow cannoning into his stomach. Air blasted from his mouth, and his torso bent forward at a right angle.

The impact of elbow to breadbasket felt good—a solid, satisfying *thunk*. Smoky was moaning and rolling as I surged to my feet. Moustache was on his knees, clutching his broken ball, mouthing something at me. I leaned in, trying to catch the word, but through his gritted agony I couldn't make it out. Was it bitch? Whore? Slut? Cunt? Fucking slut cunt? It didn't matter; he was one-nutted while I was standing tall.

I thought about saying something. I thought about kicking him in the jaw, hard enough to send the orange slug on his lip somersaulting into the river. But through the gin fog I held my nerve, and my principles: you don't boot a boy when he's down. I straightened my coat and left them there. When I reached the Lancer I drove to a sheltered spot on the edge of town. There I climbed into the back seat, pulled my coat over my body and let sleep suck me deep into the faded seat covers.

Δ

I wasn't always like this. You might find it hard to believe, but I used to be normal. Average childhood, business degree, the beginnings of a corporate career—I was your regular middle-class everychick. I used to flash eyes, say please, laugh, even dance (only to disco). I wasn't exactly a ray of sunshine, but I had fun, and those around me knew I was having it. There were parties, there were after-work drinks, there were friends and breakfast dates and a plan for a responsible and comfortable life. There was even a fiancé—a real shiny angel of a man. What can I say? People change. Careers fizzle. Lives twist and stall. Fiancés fuck blond HR consultants who specialise in the field of change management. Gin sneaks into your coffee, first in drops, then in waves. So I don't feel bad when I hurt a few feelings, bruise a few heads, crack a few bones. I don't feel much at all.

Δ

I woke up with sore knuckles and a head more or less in the same state it was every morning. Ice had grown in a thick white sheet over the windows and mirrors, and I was shivering under my coat. I switched on the engine and blasted heat from the musty air-conditioning vents towards the windscreen. Then I lurched outside, was greeted with an open-handed slap by the winter air, grabbed a scraper from the boot and chiselled away enough ice to let me see the road.

I got the hell out of Tunbridge.

Melaleuca. I knew of it, vaguely. Tiny place in the deep southwest, only accessible by boat, light aircraft or a serious hike. I remembered a history teacher banging on about it in school, something about it being one of the most isolated places on earth. If Charlotte wanted to hide without leaving the island, she couldn't have found anywhere better.

The remaining ice slowly melted and slid off the windscreen as I headed further down the Midlands. I knew a pilot in the capital who owed me a favour—she'd take me to Melaleuca. But before I called her I wanted to make sure

Charlotte had made it there. The last thing I wanted to do was fly to the end of the earth and find nothing but a few lonely wombats. The most obvious course of action was to scope out Franklin. Nobody had told the cops anything when they'd investigated, but small towns have a habit of keeping quiet.

The Midlands droned on, denuded hill after denuded hill, until I rolled into sprawling suburbs around noon. Here's a list of the places I'd choose to visit before the capital: hell, anywhere tropical, the Mariana Trench, a deeper pit of hell, my mother's house. I'd once built a life there, but now it held nothing for me but grime, anger, and the taste of dust and sick. For all its size and opportunity all it contained was people, and the associated greed, horror and dirt of people, in greater numbers than anywhere else within a thousand kilometres. After I dropkicked my corporate career to the kerb I'd stayed there for another decade, ten years of sleuthing, drinking and fucking my life up, before I finally got together with the Lancer and left the capital and its people behind.

And in case you hadn't guessed, yeah—it was pretty. The place was lousy with harbours and views and mountains and sunsets. It was enough to put a woman off her gin.

I pushed through the outer suburbs, weaving between the traffic, ignoring the docks and yachts and throngs of tourists disembarking from their cruises. Snow winked down from the looming mountain. Sunlight played across the winter water. Awful. But I made it; soon I was pushing up onto the Southern Outlet and rolling further south. As I curled inland my phone rang. I glanced at the screen and saw the flashing green name of Graham Malik. I picked up.

*Graham.*

*Yeah. How's the search going?* He sounded anxious. I could hear it in the trip of his consonants.

*Good.* I kept my tone flat. *Got a bit out of those goons who'd gone after her in Tunbridge. How's Patricia?*

*Bovine, mate. She's gone full cow. Now she wants the Range Rover. Anyway.* A breath, and a pause. *About the father.*

Like a jolt of electricity I felt it: my twinge. It rocketed through me, bouncing my skin and flailing my limbs. My hands slapped against the wheel and I nearly crashed into the metal safety barrier that hugged the highway. Then it was gone, as quickly as it arrived. I found my voice. *What about him?*

*I did a bit of digging. I'm not the best digger—you know that—but I'm not bad. And I couldn't find anything. He's got a driver's licence, but that's it. No birth certificate, no listed parents or siblings, no work history. I even checked the immigration and citizenship records—nothing there either. I haven't even found his maiden name.*

*What?*

*McAllister was the mother's name. He took it when they married.*

*So it's a forged identity.* I didn't get what he was aiming at, but the muscle memory of the twinge was still numbing my fingers. *He's not the first person to do it.*

Graham panted on. *Yeah, I know. But…I dunno, mate.*

*There's another thing. Nobody's seen him since about the same time his daughter went AWOL. I don't think he snatched her or anything—people have seen her travelling alone—but it feels off. This guy has been a part of the community for years now. Nobody's ever questioned who he is or where he's from. Ask anyone who's met him and they say how good a bloke he is, but if you pay attention, they can't say anything concrete about him. They just say he looks ordinary, acts normal, and that they can't imagine why a policeman would be interested in him. Then their eyes glaze over and they start talking about the footy or the weather.*

The world around me was turning greener; the road was curving and narrowing. I still couldn't see his point. *So I should be careful because people like him?*

*No. I'm just telling you what I dug up.* Petulance entered his voice. *I didn't have to call you. I've got shit going on, you know.*

*I know. Sorry.*

*Yeah, well. Anyway.* He relaxed—people didn't apologise to him very often. *Something's off with this. Just keep it in mind.*

*Okay. I will. Thank you.*

*You're welcome. I've gotta go get a few boxes before Patricia changes the locks.*

*All right, Graham. Good luck.*

*You too.* He hung up, and I tossed the phone onto the passenger seat as my guts went subterranean. Graham was right: there was something off about the father. I couldn't put it together in my head, but there was something more to it than a fake identity. Graham's instincts were rarely wrong, and I believed his anxieties even more than I believed his tips. And even if I thought he was full of shit, there was my twinge—that alone was enough proof that something was wrong with Charlotte's father.

But there wasn't much I could about it right now. I filed it away and tried to focus on the road.

An hour later, and the Lancer and I were in Franklin. I'm not the best detective in the world, but I know how to find the right people to answer my questions. I nosed around town for a bit, getting a feel for the locals, the work, the attitudes. Pretty soon I didn't need anyone to tell me that my answers lay at the docks. There was no airfield, so if Charlotte had gone to Melaleuca from here, it was surely by boat.

Two wharfies directed me to a yacht that had paint peeling off it in wide, curling strips. It seemed abandoned, but the sails looked recently patched, so I hammered on the door of the cabin. A few minutes later something that looked like an old sailor yanked open the portal and stumbled out to meet me. Staring through a mess of grey whiskers was a suspicious glare. I tried on a smile. *Afternoon. I'm hoping you can help me.*

*Unlikely.* His voice, coughed-up and throaty, was as rough as his craft. I clenched my smile and pushed on.

*Do you know a girl named Charlotte McAllister?* I held out the photo her brother had given me.

He kept looking at me, ignoring the picture as he spat an orb of grey-green mucus into the river. *Don't know any girls.*

I dropped the smile. *No girls that wanted to get to Melaleuca?*

He leered. *Why would a pretty girl want to go there?*

*So she's pretty.*

His eyelids narrowed in anger. He was about to retreat into his cabin when I said, softly, *I'm not a cop. I'm just someone her family has hired to find her. They're worried.* I spread my palms flat and wide. A supplicant's stance. *I can help her.*

*The girl needs no help.* He held onto the door handle, but he didn't go inside.

*I'm sure she doesn't. But she might need a friend.* I pulled a couple of fifties from my pocket. *Every now and then, we all need friends.*

He glanced at the money. He glanced up at my face. Then he dragged his fingers through his beard, heaved air into his lungs and told me everything he knew.

Δ

The sound of the Jabiru's engine churned through my ears as the verdant wilds of the southwest sprawled out beneath me. After speaking to the sailor I'd driven back to the capital and arranged to meet Cindy, the pilot I knew. A few years back she'd been involved with a man who liked bouncing her head off the fridge as foreplay. Most girls would've left, but Cindy didn't. Instead, she called me.

I persuaded the boyfriend to leave her alone—not without one or two instances of dislocated kneecaps, I should admit. Afterwards I hadn't let her pay me. I'd seen it as a civic duty.

And another, shadier part of me had seen her single-engine Jabiru as a favour I might one day need. So when I'd called her—driving while using my phone, twice in one day—she'd dropped everything and fired up the propeller. By the time I arrived she was waiting on the runway.

We buzzed on, covering forests, streams, mountains. Roads had disappeared from view an hour after take-off. Now, thirty minutes from the landing strip at Melaleuca, there were trees in every direction, except for the west, where on the horizon I could see only the shining blue haze of the Great Southern Ocean. The Jabiru's engine was too loud to allow talking, so we just stared at the view. Cindy gripped the stick, and I tried to figure out what I'd say to Charlotte when I found her.

Before our eyes a river bled out into a huge estuary, the great blue-brown bay of Bathurst Harbour, big enough to hold a city. On one edge lay a few huts and the white scar of a rudimentary landing strip. Mountains of glinting white rock ringed the flatlands in from the north. It was spectacular, I suppose, in the way that nature often is, but my attention was gripped by something else: a huge, jet-black, still-smoking field of burnt heathland. I saw Cindy gasp: *Oh my god. The farm.* Before I could ask we were descending, bumping and lurching through the air in a frenzied dive before landing roughly on the white strip of soil.

Cindy switched the engines off and went straight for the huts. *I've got to call the ranger*, she said. I followed her, but instead of moving towards the buildings I was drawn to the field of burning earth. In a few minutes my boots were toeing at the charcoal and wisps of smoke were snaking into my nostrils. It must have stretched for ten, twenty kilometres, all ash and blackness, but the surrounding area was still green. In the distance I could see the black bones of a shed, standing small and frail in the wind.

The unharmed borders of the field gave me hope: if the surrounding forests had survived the fire, there was a good chance the girl had, too. I turned back to the landing strip and huts, ready to begin my search—but a person was already walking towards me. It wasn't Cindy, and it wasn't Charlotte McAllister.

The man was approaching from the edge of the heathland, carrying a large backpack. As he came closer I could tell that he was of average height, average size: his posture held a relaxed, average kind of demeanour. Beyond this I find it hard to describe him. Even now, after all I've seen this man do, after all I know he's capable of, I can't put my finger on his features. I could say that he had a short, light-brown beard, but that might not be true; it might have been a moustache, and that moustache might have been black. Or he might have been clean-shaven, even after emerging from the bush. His hair was long, or it was shoulder-length, or neat and short, or his head was glistening with baldness. His eyes were definitely blue when they weren't green or grey, and his teeth were white and straight except when they were yellow and bent. His nose: a small, delicate thing that was somehow also large and hooked. His skin was brown when it wasn't white or grey. It was so distracting that I didn't notice the rollicking, electrifying twinge that was shaking me from head to toe.

I stood still, burnt vegetation crackling under my boots. When he was within a few feet of me he stopped, his eyes roving over the smoking field. He spoke, in a voice that was rich-bold-quiet-calm. *Bad sight.*

I folded my arms. *In a certain light I'm quite appealing.*

He smiled. His eyes lifted from the black landscape and settled on my face. These eyes—shifting, unknowable points of whiteness and iris and heat—froze me to the ground. I had questions for him; I had plenty; but I couldn't get them out. My thoughts started spinning, and my tongue turned fat and numb. He stared on, and though his body didn't move he came closer to me. It felt like his eyes were touching my own, sharing fluid, bumping pupils, until finally I heaved myself out of this funk and half-shouted: *Who are you?*

His eyes finally slid off mine, and I felt a rushing, deeply physical sense of relief as he said: *I think you know.* He inhaled, rubbed his face, turned around and began slowly trudging in the direction he had come from.

After he'd walked thirty or so metres whatever had been pinning me to the spot let go. I shook off the lethargy and began following him, fists tight, ready to beat the answers out of him if I had to; but as I neared him he stopped, and I stopped too, not of my own accord. My feet, again, snapped still. He spoke without turning, in a voice I can't remember but with words I won't forget. *Stay away from my daughter.*

With that he walked on, trudging across the plain. I

thought about going after him again, but what was the point? The sight of his shrinking back, changing colour and shape before my eyes even from this distance, drew a curtain of exhaustion over me. I blinked, swayed on my feet, realised how tired I was. How steadily my hangover was hammering at my temples. How far away I was from home. I wondered what my neighbour's tom was doing, if it was on my couch, picking at the ham I'd probably left out. I was hollowed out and hungry. I would've killed for a decent sandwich, but food wasn't the answer; it never was. I reached into the folds of my coat, fumbling for the bottle I knew wasn't there. I'd come too far on a bad case. I'd been hit on by creeps and bewitched by a bushwalker, and I hadn't found the McAllister girl. The dim peal of failure rang between my ears. The only thing that would make me feel better was a tall glass of my burning best friend, and I was all out of gin.

# FEATHER

*The following entries are taken from the diary of Allen Gibson, manager of the Melaleuca Farm Estate.*

## ONE

Something is killing the wombats. We found the first corpse three weeks ago. Since then there have been nine more, and the rate is increasing. Their deaths have clearly come about through some kind of unnatural molestation. Something has torn at their throats and underbellies, leaving violet holes in their fur, and in every case their eyes have been plucked clean from their sockets. The nature of these injuries points to the culprit being some kind of bird—each wound I have found could only have been caused by the stab of a beak or bill—but there are no birds here that could inflict such horrendous wounds on a creature as powerful as a wombat. Perhaps a wedge-tailed eagle could do it, if starving and desperate, but it is highly unlikely. And in any case, an eagle would feast upon a dead wombat until it was too heavy to fly. It would never leave its kill to be found by a farmer.

Other than the usual clamour of seabirds, ravens and swamp harriers, the only other birds of note in this area are orange-bellied parrots—gorgeous, high-squawking, stupid creatures that migrate north every year—and a few black-faced cormorants that venture up from the tannin-stained waters of Bathurst Harbour. The largest of these lives in a blackwood tree that stands alone in a far field, above the grave of the farm's founder, Derek Quorn. It is a territorial creature, often harassing our livestock if they stray into its paddock, but to my knowledge it has never so much as drawn blood from a wombat. I do not like to go near it, partly because I find the bird loathsome, but also because Old Quorn's paddock contains the main shaft of the old Melaleuca tin mine. Any number of other shafts and sinkholes may have been obscured by the meadows of buttongrass. It would be easy to fall through such a trap, and it could take years before anyone found you.

The other cormorants in the area show no interest in the activities of the farm—and even if they were acting out of the ordinary, the wounds I've found have been far too large to be the work of a cormorant's bill. The parrots, meanwhile, are incapable of harming anything other than themselves.

Logic points to the killer being human, but the only people here are the two farmhands, Nicola and Charlotte, and myself. The park ranger visits every so often and a pilot drops off supplies once a month, but other than that it is just the three of us. The situation is perplexing and upsetting—I must admit that the deaths are taking a significant toll on me. Over the years I have formed a strong bond with the wombats. It is hard to explain, but if you have seen one and admired its friendly face, its amiable trot or its marvellous thick coat, you might begin to understand what it is like to raise these creatures from the moment they emerge from their mother's pouch. Having failed to meet the right woman I do not have children of my own, and this herd of wombats is the closest thing to family that I might ever know.

Obviously I am not killing the creatures, but I cannot bring myself to believe that either of the women is doing it—especially Nicola. In her second winter with us she has proven to be the most reliable hand the farm has ever hired. Hard-working, capable and diligent, she also displays a level of care and affection for the livestock that I have never seen in my twenty-odd years of farming. It's hard to believe that she has come to us all the way from the north coast; it is as if she had been born here. She is as close to the wombats as I am. I have no doubt that she will make a fine vet once she has finished university, although she will need to toughen up. Each time we find a new corpse she cannot help but weep, and the anguish in her expression often inspires in me an intense feeling of despair.

I suppose if you were to suspect one of us, it would be Charlotte, the new hand—but, hard as I try, I cannot convince myself that she is responsible. Yes, behind her pale face there lurks a curious ferocity; and yes, she often wanders through the freezing fields alone after her work for the day is done; and yes, she occasionally seems to lose control of herself in fits of quiet emotion, eyes closed, hands clenched, small noises leaking through her gritted teeth. But it cannot be her; she loves the wombats more than Nicola does, if that were possible. After checking their skin for ticks every morning she brushes them, an inessential task that she revels in, murmuring in their ears, ruffling their necks as if they were pets. In the afternoons she watches over them so intently that I worry for the health of her eyes. And in the evenings she shepherds them into their burrows with a wordless song that lulls them into a state of hypnosis; as she sings they march sleepily towards her voice and tumble into their holes, more placid than I have ever seen them. While Nicola cries over the fresh corpses, Charlotte cannot look at them; she retreats to the farthest part of the farm to scream, and scream, and scream. Her care is as obvious as it is distressing. It cannot be her.

I do not believe there is yet a need to contact Mrs Quorn, the owner of the farm. She has left the property in my care for nearly a decade now, and I would hate to give her a reason to doubt my reliability. It's possible that she would want to come and see the corpses for herself. Or worse—she might fire me. I cannot bear the thought of being taken away from the farm, or from Melaleuca. If the wombats are my family, then this place is my home. Its undulating moorlands of peat and buttongrass; the glints of white quartzite that blink on the mountain caps; the cold, clean welcome of its unbroken sky; the harsh cliffs and tea-coloured waters; the gathering sense of wild solitude that breathes out of every crack in the land. I cannot go back to the flat brown farms of the Midlands, or the over lush dairy pastures of the northwest. I won't be leaving the lonely beauty of this place; not if I can help it.

In any case, the hands and I have come up with a plan: like shepherds of old we will begin sleeping among our flock, taking turns to stay up all night beside the vulnerable burrows. This will surely help us catch the killer, although I am aware that it will play havoc with my already troubled sleep. For weeks I have been unable to find sufficient rest. I have been lying awake, my mind plagued by images of the wombat corpses, and what sleep I have been snatching has been filled with inky shadows and surging fears that I can never recall in any detail. Still, it cannot be avoided. And besides—these nightly distresses are surely being caused by the dying animals. As soon as they are safe, I'm sure my sleep shall return to its normal state.

## TWO

Our plan to safeguard the wombats at night seemed to be working. While we did not catch whatever has been killing them, neither did any more wombats die for the first six nights of our vigil. A sense of cautious optimism began permeating the farm. Perhaps the killer had been a wild dog that, now faced with our presence, had decided to move on? This story became more convincing after every successful watch, and by the seventh night—my third turn to act as watchman—I was half-convinced that the threat had disappeared. Perhaps this was why I let my concentration slip. By two o'clock a sense of weariness came over me, and after such a long time without a proper sleep I did not have the strength to resist it. I remember my head nodding forward, but instead of finally experiencing the deep sleep my body had promised I was again visited by the dark, flickering dreams that have been my nightly companions for weeks. These shapes sent a nameless horror clattering through my soul, even as I lay dead to the world under my fleece parka.

At daybreak I awoke with a sudden lurch, slumped at my post, exhausted and thankful to be free of the dreams. I looked around, seeing the wombats happily emerging from their subterranean lairs, and felt a tremendous sense of relief. They were only waking up; none had been harmed. But as I stood and stretched and flexed my fingers against the cold I saw them ambling in a wide, strange pattern, avoiding a low part of the paddock just beyond the mouths of their burrows. With apprehension churning through me I wandered over to find not one but three dead wombats lying in a neat line. The wounds were identical to the previous victims, and their eyes, of course, had been neatly removed. Horror even greater than I'd felt in my dreams overcame me, but it was soon replaced by fury—at myself; at whatever was responsible; and, for the first time in a decade, at Melaleuca, for being so isolated and primitive. At some point grief crept into me too, I am sure, although my memories of its cold touch are obscured by the red rage that was swelling inside me.

Needless to say, the hands were grievously upset when I told them what had happened. Nicola tried to maintain a brave face, but I could see that these killings had affected her more than all of the others combined. Charlotte did not attempt to conceal her reaction. A howl of despair burst forth from her mouth, right there in front of us, a howl not aimed at me or my laxness or at anything in particular: a torn, broken howl.

We buried the bodies and tried to get on with the farm work. I confess that it was hard, perhaps the hardest day I have ever spent on the land. But I refuse to give up hope. Far worse things have been happening to farms and farmers all over the world for thousands of years. Floods, fire, pestilence, disease; yet farmers always find a way to push on. I will not let a few dead marsupials conquer my spirit.

### THREE

Hope has appeared, although not in the form any of us expected. The most recent wombat corpse—there have been six more since I last wrote—was accompanied by a number of midnight-black feathers that could only belong to a black-faced cormorant. Their abnormal size told me that they must have fallen from the wings of the huge specimen that lives in Old Quorn's burial field.

We had finally learned who the killer was! But the hands were not as relieved as I had expected them to be. If anything, the feathers only increased the gloom and mistrust that has been hovering over them for the last week. It is as if they have given up hope, or as if—and this is surely impossible, no matter how many times the thought occurs to me—they are blaming me for what has happened. I am quite sure that I can see their eyes narrowing every time I wander past them in the yard or wave to them in the field from my quad bike. It is true that these troubling times have brought them closer; their dining chairs practically bump legs at the table, and it has become a rare sight to see them alone. I do not like this closeness. I feel that they are gossiping, murmuring false-hoods about me, plotting to abandon the farm and accuse me of misdeeds. Where once I admired them, now I regard them with suspicion.

Still, they are performing their duties adequately, even though the herd is suffering, and not only from the drop in numbers—the remaining wombats have gone off their grass. Almost all of them are now small enough to allow their ribs to poke out against the dull folds of their usually lustrous fur. Instances of ticks, fleas and mange are also rising, and caring for this reduced number of creatures is more work than the large, healthy herd ever was.

It is obvious to me that the loss of stock, combined with the ill-health of the remaining beasts, means that we will not be able to meet our orders by the end of the season. We had agreed to supply over five hundred premium-grade pelts to various clients, but at this rate we will be lucky to harvest even half that number. I know that I need to tell Mrs Quorn—and I know that she will be unlikely to retain my services once she discovers what has been going on—but I cannot bring myself to tell her of the problem without first having solved it. And with these feathers, I finally have a way to do so. Once I have killed the monstrous cormorant I will telephone her immediately.

Another thing: since I found the feathers my dreams have changed. They are still visiting me, every night, and they still contain the flickering, shifting tongues of murky darkness, yet they have been robbed of their menace. I no longer feel horror when they swamp my sleeping mind, only curiosity.

## FOUR

It has been years since I last hunted, so I am trying to be forgiving of myself. But my inability to catch the cormorant is as confounding as it is vexing. For the past six mornings I have ventured out into its field, armed with a shotgun, net and knife, and each trip has been an utter failure. I can find the bird without any trouble—it is never far from its home, the looming blackwood—but somehow it always evades me. It sits in the upper branches, huge and silent, preening its cloud-white chest with its dagger of a bill, paying no attention to me other than the occasional flick of a sharp eye. But as soon as I take aim it trades perches, hopping up, down, left and right, every time I try to get a sight on it. At no point does the creature seem perturbed. If anything, the glint in its eye is one of humour.

If I try to force it lower it descends only far enough to trick me into leaping, casting my net and getting it caught on the branches. Occasionally it takes wing and flaps to a fence post on the other side of the field. On more than one occasion this has tempted me into firing after it, my gun booming a scatter of pellets that never even graze the webbing of its feet. I am often tempted to pursue it on foot, but I dare not risk going near the abandoned mine. Its rusting maw gapes at me from across the field, and I think the cormorant can sense my fear. Once landed it turns, beholds me with its pointy eyes and releases its high harsh cry, which has followed me out of the paddock every afternoon for the last six days—a cry I cannot mute or halt or escape.

I am being toyed with: that much is certain. And even more frustrating than my inability to kill the beast is the fact that the wombats are still dying. Each morning reveals a new victim. Now that we have reached the dead of winter frost has begun snapping in pink-white sheets across their wounds, forming ice webs over the frozen blood and viscera. It is tempting to believe that the monstrous cormorant has taken revenge on my harassments by increasing its quota of kills, but it seems just as likely that other cormorants—its minions, perhaps—are responsible. More of them have been arriving on the property with every passing day, abandoning the harbour for reasons I cannot explain. Their feathers have begun to scatter in great numbers across the fields, black quills darkening the grass and frost and intermittent snow.

This assault of plumage has taken a toll on the hands. Each time they see a fresh feather they shudder and turn away, so I have taken to collecting them and storing them in my room, away from where Nicola or Charlotte will see them. But all this cringing, this flinching—it is not fitting for professional farmhands to behave in such a manner. And their attachment to the wombats, once such a benefit to the farm, is now a sappy and enraging show of foolishness. They simper after the herd, cooing and frowning at the skinny beasts, treating them as if they were sick children, not mind-less marsupials. They are certainly no help in dealing with what is actually threatening them. Each morning I march off, gun in hand and knife in belt, as their eyes follow me filled with what looks more and more like fear. It is futile, feminine softness, and nothing more. I am beginning to regret hiring them.

I can kill the monstrous cormorant. Of this I am sure. Yet the longer I hunt it, the less angry I become at my failure. Initially it was infuriating, but lately I have caught myself studying the creature for nearly an hour without even raising my gun. There is a calculated wisdom in its black stare; or if not wisdom, a depth, an intensity, a kind of primitive under-standing of things; and my respect for it grows each day. I would write more, but I am exhausted. Sleep is calling me. At least this is something I can rely on—for as tough as life has become, recently my sleep has never been better.

## FIVE

To describe what I saw in my sleep last night as dreams would be like calling a whale a fish, a storm a cloud. What I had were *visions*. As soon as my head hit the pillow my mind was swamped with the dark, flickering shapes that I have become well used to, yet never before have they been so clear. Their nameless murk had transformed into sharp imagery that reared before me, bold, violent and profound. As I watched them, in this newfound clarity, I saw that they were more than just shapes: they were creatures. And not just creatures: birds. And not just birds: as they wheeled through the hazy sky I made out the shapes of their wings, the cruel hooks of their bills, the pale shading of their chests against the hard blackness of their backs, and suddenly I saw they were cormorants, hundreds of cormorants, thousands of cormorants, all careering in a whirling dance before me. Below them I saw that the shrouded landscape was not a bare dreamfield but a version of the farm, cast in twilight, with the wilds of Melaleuca turned grey instead of green. Here there were no wombats, no fences, no meddling contraptions of machinery or human design. Only cormorants, and quietness, and for some reason, me.

I waited for them to turn on me, strangely unafraid of the death they carried in their bills, yet they did not. Then I realised: this flying dance was not a threat, but a message of acknowledgment, or acceptance, or even friendship. They had been trying to tell me this ever since my dreams began—that we were close, somehow, and should be closer. It dawned over me like a crashing tide, knowledge that felt powerful and immense: I was *welcome* here. My dream-self turned weak and watery. And when the realisation had seeped right through me, from my forehead to my toes, I saw into the centre of the flock of birds, straight at a figure I had not previously seen, a figure they were circling. A single huge member of their species, sitting still and calm on a black-wood branch: the monstrous cormorant of Old Quorn's field. Through the vortex of shadows and feathers it was branding me with a muscled, soulful stare. It opened its bill and, just as the first note of its high cry screamed across the twilight field and into my ears, I woke up.

Light had filled my room through the small window. The smell of salt and oil was thick in the air. Usually after I awoke I would be groggy and disoriented, but this day I had never felt more alert. Rolling over I saw that I had somehow gone to sleep on the pile of cormorant feathers that I have been collecting over the past few days. I couldn't remember placing them on my bed before I fell asleep, but this seemed unimportant.

I got dressed, washed my face and headed outside into the fields. I didn't know what time it was. It must have been around dusk, because I could hear Charlotte singing the wombats into their burrows. Her lilting, wordless ramble scratched at my ears. Its docile tone reminded me of her stupidity, of her pointless quest to care for these wretched beasts. Couldn't she see that they were doomed? I watched them lumber towards her, four-legged lumps of uselessness made flesh, and realised that I hated them, that I must always have hated them, that I had been lying to myself for all the long years I have been trapped in this barren southern hell.

## SIX

Damn these women! Damn them! They have contacted the ranger without my permission, telling him uncounted lies and exaggerations about the business on the farm. He arrived here this morning, full of questions and concerns, as if I had done something wrong. I was roused from the depth of my murky visions by his knocking and shouting, and was in mind to turn my shotgun on him. Perhaps I should have. Or perhaps I should have aimed at those feeble, treacherous women. How I hate them; oh, how I wish them pain.

The ranger had taken it upon himself to tour the farm without me, no doubt encouraged by Nicola and Charlotte. I glared as he fumbled through his inane questions—about the farm, the wombats; about me, if I was feeling unwell, did I need to see a doctor, did Mrs Quorn know, what was my plan, why hadn't I contacted anyone, et cetera, all in a wheedling, faux-friendly tone. A jellyfish of a man. I can't remember exactly what I told him, but my words must have been harsh, for after I responded to his lengthy ramble he finally rediscovered his spine. It straightened, pushing his chest outwards so that his toy-like badge glinted in the weak sunlight, as he told me that I needed to do something—fast, and alone. For the hands, he claimed, had asked him to organise them a flight out. They were resigning, the buffoon told me, and did not feel like they could tell me to my face. They were scared, he said, scared of me and scared for me. And so was he: in his pink face I could see the concern of a simpleton. *You aren't yourself*, he said. *Let me give you a hand and we'll sort all this out.*

I have known the ranger for many years. In the past he would come to the farm for dinner, or I would pop into his hut for a glass of whisky, whenever he had cause to be in Melaleuca. Ending a friendship like ours is usually a painful experience, yet I felt nothing as I told him to leave the farm and never return. I felt even less as I grabbed my shotgun and marched towards him, yelling words that I cannot recall. But that is a lie: I did feel something. I felt joy. I felt power. I felt the giddy swirl of freedom.

He fled, as all cowards do, and I did not listen to the words he left hanging in the driveway air. The hands, too, had disappeared. And lucky for them that they did, for my shotgun had both barrels loaded, and I doubt that I would have hesitated to fire. At the sight of the empty farm—empty, that is, save for the remaining gaggle of insipid wombats and the black-and-white shapes of the cormorants—I exhaled, long and slow. A feeling of calmness settled over me. Control, finally, had been restored. I went back inside, ate a simple meal and returned to my bed, which was now covered in a layer of cormorant feathers so thick that I couldn't see the blankets beneath them.

Before I allowed myself to sink into my visions, I decided to go back to Old Quorn's field as soon as I woke up. I would visit the leader of the cormorants, and then I would know how next to proceed. I knew this was the right course of action to take; I cannot explain how, but it was. He would show me the path.

## SEVEN

Forgive me if I cannot finish this entry—I am in tremendous pain, and am struggling to grip my pen. Yet I regret nothing, except how long it has taken me to finally understand— to see the truth of what has been happening. To put it simply, something remarkable has happened. Something wonderful.

When I woke from my sleep after the ranger visited I set out to see the glorious cormorant of Old Quorn's field. I did not take my gun or net—as I strode it seemed absurd to me that I ever had—but I did slide my knife into my belt: an old farm habit. I also brought this journal with me, in case the cormorant communicated something to me that I needed to record. As I walked I passed the dwindling herd of wombats, not even letting my hatred of them put a kink in my spirits. Melaleuca had never looked so grand. The frost was carpeting the meadows and moorlands, dropping a crust of pure whiteness onto the green thumbs of grass, and the mountains all around were dusted with snow a sharper white than the gritty quartzite peaks they were covering.

Bathurst Harbour stretched out to the northwest, its navy waters stained red-brown by the tannins leaking from the highland streams. I felt as if the world was open to me, and that my troubles were receding into the distance at a furious canter.

When I reached the field I did not see the cormorant. This was odd—he was always there, roosting in the branches of the blackwood—but I did not fret. He was no doubt out fishing. I sat down at the base of the tree, leaning against its trunk, and waited patiently as minutes and then hours began to pass by. The sun rose and fell in its low winter arc as I shivered into my wool coat. Eventually I fell asleep, which was the key; I should have known it. As soon as my mind plummeted into unconsciousness he appeared. Behind my eyelids he swooped downwards, coming straight at me through a black sky, a missile of feathers and darkness and baleful eyes, and the joy I felt at his presence was the richest moment of happiness I have ever experienced. He flew closer, and although it was hard to judge the distance in this dream-vision I felt that he was about to waft his glorious feathers across my face. The anticipation was excruciating; in that moment I wanted nothing more than to be in his presence, to feel his touch. And just as it finally happened, just as his bill was about to plunge into my chest and soul, I awoke.

But this awakening was not caused by him: I had been awoken by something else, a nudging feeling somewhere near my shins. I looked down to see a wombat staring up at me. It was a particularly ugly specimen, all ribs and snot and sick, patchy fur. Again it nosed at my shin, whimpering out a low note of sorrow, wanting I don't know what, and my confusion was swiftly replaced with implacable fury. Before I knew what I was doing I had risen to my feet, kicked the creature onto its back, drawn the knife from my belt, and plunged it hard and deep into its mangy chest.

As my knife entered its body, I knew. I knew so deeply and completely what had happened that I fell to my knees. The surging pulse of knowledge began in the wombat's slowing heart and flew upwards, through the knife, through my arm, through my veins and lungs and flesh and up into my brain, triggering the memories—of all the times I'd done it before. I reeled backwards as the memories asserted themselves. I saw the first time, when I'd wandered in my sleep out into the fields, groggily dragging a beast from its burrow and stabbing it, zombie-like, before ripping out its eyes and leaving it to die on the cold grass. Then I remembered the next times, as my gait had become firmer and my arm stronger, going straight for the burrows and killing with firm purpose. Then more, as I grew in confidence, as I took unconscious pleasure in the killing, laughing to myself as I happily stabbed at fur and flesh and bone, as my mind was swamped by dark shadows of flying cormorants. All of it came to me, all clear and all at once, and once I knew it I could not forget it.

A knocking. A scraping. A needling, pointing dig of a bill at my chest, not on the outside of it but from the inner walls, behind my skin and sternum. I stood up, grabbing at myself, trying to figure out what was happening even as the wombat-murdering memories blared through my mind. A high harsh cry sounded somewhere. I turned around, looking from fence to tree to tin mine, but there was no bird. No glorious cormorant. The needling and knocking continued, sharper and harder. My hand flew back to my chest. The cry pealed out again, only now I could tell that it was not assaulting my ears from the outside, but from between them. And then I knew—the dream had not been cut short. The glorious cormorant did reach me; it touched me; it *joined* with me. It had entered within the cage of my flesh. If I doubted it for one second I needed only to feel for the stabbing bill inside my chest or listen for the rasping cry between my ears. And I needed only to look to my right, which I did, for my eye was caught by a scene I shall not rhapsodise but merely describe: hundreds upon hundreds of cormorants, flying at great pace out of the mouth of the old tin mine, blackening the world around me with their furious wings. The clean sky turned white and black. Joy filled my shared heart. As they rose and swirled and called to me the needling bill pushed, and the cutting bird-scream told: we were not yet done with death.

I strode through the field, clutching my knife, directed by the tapping of the bill on my breastbone. Night had dropped over Melaleuca. I could no longer make out the white caps of the mountains or the glinting frost of the grass. The blue-red-brown waters of Bathurst Harbour, too, were lost to me. But the glorious cormorant was not worried, and neither was I.

Soon I made it to the burrows, where the wombats were stumbling in circles around the mouths of their dens. I went straight for the one closest to me, knife in hand. The glorious cormorant shrieked with delight as my free palm smacked into the creature's neck fur. I flipped the beast over. Its stumpy legs wobbled in the air. I think ticks had burrowed into its face, because it showed no recognition of me, or of anything; it just barked in surprise and confusion. I realised with dismay that it wouldn't even see its death coming, that I wouldn't see fear in its eyes as my arm descended. But the cormorant didn't care—it wanted only to see the wombat's blood. Its bill was tapping harder than ever, a staccato fury of pecks. The knife was hot and eager in my grasp. I bent down, raised the blade, and was aiming at the wombat's throat when I heard a human scream.

Nicola. I straightened, shocked, and nearly dropped my knife. She was standing at the top of the field. In the gloom I could see her whole body shaking, horror and fear smeared across her face. She screamed again, this time using my name—*Allen!* She said other words, too, but I didn't make them out, couldn't understand, didn't want to, because now I was walking towards her. The thrumming peck of the cormorant's bill was leading me her way, and I was still holding the knife in a high, overhand grip. Nicola began backing away, but I was moving fast—it felt like the glorious cormorant's wings were fanning at the back of my knees, lending me unnatural speed.

I didn't think about what I was doing; there was no

need to think. She would not be able to get away. But then another voice echoed across the meadow—a female voice, like Nicola's, but mixed with more fury than fear. I looked in the direction of the farmhouse, where it had come from, and saw Charlotte springing towards me. Through the hazy light she ran, straight towards me, and the cormorant and I switched our focus: we would kill her first. The other cormorants, wheeling in the sky above us, agreed with our decision. Their cries fell down, urging us on.

The glorious cormorant and I stalked forward, knife ready, as Charlotte sprinted downhill. She was a mess of angry angles, flailing wildly, and her rangy stride beckoned me forward. I began running, powered by the thirst of my other feathered half, and that was when I saw it. I still can't believe I saw it; I can't believe I am writing this down; yet it was what happened.

Charlotte yelled, something violent and wordless. And as she yelled, a blue light began leaking from her eyes. Her ears, too—and her nostrils. Six trails of glowing ultra-blueness were running down her face, to be joined by two more that spurted out of the sides of her mouth, making eight lines of unnatural colour. These streams began falling to the ground, and I saw that ten more lines were also cascading out of her hands from beneath her fingertips. Blue, hyper-blue, and when all these too-blue trails hit the buttongrass it took only a few seconds for the acrid smell of smoke to reach me. I realised, too late: it was not liquid leaking from Charlotte McAllister; it was fire.

Nicola ran forward. Charlotte's flames were spreading around her feet, and it was only then that she realised what was happening. I think she was as surprised as I was. All four of us standing there—Charlotte, Nicola, myself and the glorious cormorant—were momentarily frozen by this incredible sight…but then the grass licked up in a sudden crackle of fire. Blue flames jumped, swayed, grew. The grass was wet, but Charlotte could not stop leaking. Her spurts increased, and as she panicked she shook her arms, spreading the fire further. She looked at me then, through her burning eyes, and I knew, even through the tapping of the cormorant's bloodthirsty bill, that if I wanted to live I needed to run.

I sprinted towards Old Quorn's field. Sparks were flying through the air, hot and incandescent, and I felt them settle in my hair, on my coat, on my hands. My flesh began to cook, and a bright agony caught hold of me, but I kept running. I looked over my shoulder to see Charlotte chasing me. Fire was pouring down her chin and chest in a cascade of burning vomit. Rolling walls of cornflower flames were sprinting past her, nipping at my feet, and even with my wing-enhanced legs I could not outrun them. The fire caught me, and I burned hotter. The pain was enough to make me scream, and as I did so the glorious cormorant joined in. Our cries burst forth into the Melaleuca sky, but I did not stop running.

When I reached the field I felt the cormorant calm at the sight of its blackwood tree, but I did not, for I know what fire does to trees, so I kept running, even though a quick glance showed me that Charlotte had stopped chasing. I ran to the last place I ever thought I'd go. Blue fire licked my skin, and I ran and ran and threw myself, headfirst, into the open sore of the old tin mine.

## EIGHT

Before these events, I wasn't much of a writer. Jotting down my thoughts had seemed unnecessary and self-indulgent. Yet, aside from my great friend the glorious cormorant, writing has been the only thing that has gotten me through this alarming period of my life. It is odd to think of what I would have done without it.

It has now been a week since I plunged into the mine (or something like a week—time down here does not seem all that important). My injuries from the fire were severe, yet they have healed remarkably well, especially considering that I have been squatting in a dank pool of rusty water, surrounded by nothing but dirt, feathers and rotting wood. I owe this, I am sure, to my union with the glorious cormorant. He has been healing me from within, taking care of my unworthy body.

This supercharged healing has not been without a few unexpected side effects, however. The day I plunged down here I fell into a great clump of feathers that lined the floor of the mine. As I lay there, nearly unconscious due to the pain, my burning skin fused with these feathers in some sort of flesh-to-quill welding process. A scattered layer of black plumage now sprouts from my arms and back, stuck fast by

Charlotte's fire, and for some reason the feathers do not die. If anything, they are growing larger and more lustrous.

The only other part of my body that did not heal properly was my nose. It still functions as a nose, more or less, but its shape has changed. Where once it was wide, flat and fleshy it has morphed, from the heat, into a much straighter protuberance. It has become harder too, almost bonelike, and hairs no longer sprout from my nostrils. I cannot see it very well in the gloom, but when the sun shines onto the pools of water down here I can see that it also seems much darker—as black as the pits of the abandoned tunnels around me.

But I cannot complain. The cormorants deliver fish every morning, keeping me well fed. I can even use their watery blood to write with. How lucky I am that this journal survived my journey through the flames, nestled in the breast pocket of my coat. It has not abandoned me, and neither, I am pleased to report, has my strength. My body is gaining a power it never had. And the glorious cormorant within me is content, which is more than enough to keep me happy. There are no fat marsupials for me to care for, no plotting women, no endless inanity of farm chores and duties. Here I have found the solitude that I have been searching for my whole life.

Yet it will not last. The glorious cormorant is only calm because it knows we will one day leave. Once I am strong enough we will climb out of this pit—or perhaps we will fly? Who knows how strong these feathers will grow? And what we do then he hasn't told me, but I can read the shadows of his thoughts, and I can decipher the code in the taps of his bill. His hunger persists. There will be more blood, more death, more warmth sucked up by the coldness of the night, and I will be with him, hand in feather, when it happens.

# CAKE

*Chapter 28 of* CREAM, BUTTER AND SMALL-TOWN NUTTERS: THE LIFE AND TIMES OF AN AVOCA MATRIARCH, *by Mavis Midcurrent.*

Now comes the point in my tale where I must pay homage to the wonderful people of Avoca, my home for so many years. Of course, there are too many to name, each and every one of them worthy of a paragraph or two in their own right. A town as special as Avoca is home to many special people. But I will limit myself to those who have had the greatest effect on my life; this is my story, after all.

I will begin with Larry, the pump attendant at Gherkin's Fuel & Food. Larry has been a vital friend to the community (and particularly me) for more than forty years, providing the friendliest, politest and most reliable refuelling service this side of the mountain. He's there every time you pull up, rain, hail or shine, pumping away with his trademark enthusiasm, never letting you go home dry. Larry was my husband Phillip's best man at our wedding, and was always there for our family, particularly when Phillip was working in the copper mines far away from home. I would've died of loneliness in those long, cold months if it weren't for Larry; after his shifts finished he would come straight over, keeping me company and cheering me up, as full of beans as a teenager. Larry, if you're reading this, thank you for everything. I don't know what I would have done without you. Hopefully you and Phillip patch things up soon.

Who else? Mayor Constance Tring, of course. What citizen of Avoca hasn't had their life touched by this remarkable woman? From reforming by-laws to clearing willows from the South Esk, she has been a tireless source of progress for our town, despite all the persecution she faced, simply for pursuing a career in local representation while possessing a uterus. What an inspiration she is! On a personal note, I'd like to thank the good mayor for including me on the panel of judges for the annual Avoca Beauty Pageant for the last eighteen years. The pageant, as many will know, is the only exclusively male beauty competition in the southern hemisphere, and it has been my honour and privilege to adjudicate the merits of so many of our handsome and talented young men. I would struggle immensely if I had to pick a favourite out of all the winners we judges have selected over the years, but eventually, I suppose, I would have to say that Garth Burbank stands slightly above the rest. Such poise, such cheek-bones, such a dazzling smile! And that's not even mentioning his expert skills in sheep shearing and embroidery. Garth, wherever you are, I hope you've done as well in the big wide world as we all believed you would. (And if you're ever back in Avoca, do pay me a visit—I haven't forgotten those special times you visited my cottage and convinced me of your champion qualities.)

And how could I let the lovely ladies of the Avoca chapter of the Country Women's Association go unmentioned? They've been my tribe, my sisters, through all the blessings and troubles of my life. When I was named Rural Businesswoman of the Year they were the first ones to knock on my salon door and demand fresh styles—imagine my joy at seeing such good friends celebrate my humble skill with scissors! And when Phillip and I endured that tough period during his sixth winter in the mines they were constantly by my side, sustaining me with teacake, scones and sisterly love. All of them, that is, except for Beryl Newtburg, who thought it appropriate to direct her concerns towards my estranged husband. As I have detailed in previous chapters Phillip always stayed true to me, even in the face of that so-called lady's advances. I hope you choke on a chicken bone, Beryl.

Yes, I have been wildly lucky in my Avoca friends and family. There was, however, the odd bod or two who wasn't the friendliest of characters. Isn't that always the way with small towns? I won't list every Avoca local I've ever found

uncharitable—I don't want this book to spark controversy!—
but I will make an exception in the case of Thurston Hough,
a woodworking enthusiast who moved to the area a few
years ago. (He was also an author, apparently, although no
one in town had ever heard of his 'best-selling' book.) That
man never had a kind word to say to or about anyone, and
although he was rarely seen in town he still managed to be so
unpleasant, so vile, that many people would run in the opposite direction if they ever saw him coming.

Let me give you an example: after moving to the area
it took him less than two days to make a mortal enemy of
Gladys Grapefruit, our postwoman. After receiving his first
lot of post (which included, I believe, nothing more than a
power bill and a welcome letter from the local Scout troop)
Mr Hough stormed into the post office and demanded to
know how the authorities had discovered his address. Gladys
(who, at the age of one hundred and two, was the country's
oldest public servant) told him that she was merely delivering
his mail, and Mr Hough responded with a storm of screams,
threats and general carry-on about the so-called invasion
of his privacy, before returning home and setting fire to his
letterbox. Undaunted, Gladys continued to deliver his letters
by sliding them under his front door. Mr Hough countered
her efforts by putting posters up all over town with such
slogans as EXTERMINATE ENVELOPES and GRAPEFRUIT: SOUR
FRUIT, SOUR WOMAN and RALLY AGAINST POST TERROR, THIS
SUNDAY, 3 PM. Shortly after tearing down these posters (and
celebrating her victory with a long night of sherry, bingo

and dancing), Gladys died in her sleep. Notwithstanding her advanced age, many locals believed her feud with Mr Hough was the cause of her death, and from then on he was marked as a strange character who was best left alone.

But despite the distance the townsfolk kept from Mr Hough, controversies continued to occur. He fell into the South Esk and tried to sue the water company; he got into arguments over the price of potato cakes at the fish-and-chip shop; he challenged the milkman to a duel at high noon; and on one sweltering summer's day two local lads, Garry and Barry Chinstrap, accidentally trespassed on his property while taking their motocross bikes for a ride. After spying them through his kitchen window, Mr Hough tracked them all the way to the Avoca Arms, where they were enjoying a post-ride beer, and started shooting at them with what looked like an ancient air rifle. He missed both Garry and Barry— according to them, they had never seen someone less skilled with a firearm—but he did manage to clip my poor Larry (who was having a counter lunch) on the ear. Incensed, all three of them chased Mr Hough out into the street, where Garry, Barry and Larry gave him what was described around town as a 'thorough belting'.

And do you think he learned anything? Do you think a public hiding convinced him to change his ways? If so, you are mistaken. Only days later he committed what was perhaps his worst crime of all: distributing flyers throughout the region claiming that my beloved Country Women's Association was a secret arm of the government, with the sole aim of infecting the population with mind-control chemicals, based on the fact that we do not include lists of ingredients on our homemade cakes and jams. Needless to say, my fellow women and I were shocked to our very cores, and spent hours (hours!) tracking down and destroying the ridiculous material. To this day we still get asked if our recipes include microchips or pacifying agents or uncommon levels of oestrogen.

But Avoca had the last laugh on Mr Hough. Just as we were drawing up a petition to have him banished from the municipality, a rumour began spreading through town that he had died, which was soon confirmed by the local constable. Hough's body had been discovered in his house by one of his clients. No cause of death was given, but most of us believed a heart attack or some other stress-related illness had taken him, no doubt brought about by his explosive temper and violent constitution. Relatives were searched for to identify the body, but none could be found. I wouldn't have been surprised if his family had disowned him many years ago, and besides, it wouldn't have made any difference, because Mr Hough's body had apparently been in such a state of deterioration that a visual identification would have been impossible. The local wildlife had broken into his house and gnawed upon his body—water rats, in particular, had taken a liking to him, feasting upon his toes, fingers and face.

Given the grisly nature of his passing, I suppose it would be appropriate to say something nice about Mr Hough. But I'm afraid I can't; he was a terrible neighbour, an unpleasant person and a poor citizen. Compare him to any of the upright people of Avoca (Lovely Larry! Garrulous Gladys! Gorgeous Garth!) and he is left wanting, every time. I'm sorry to say it, but the town is much better off without him. And if you think I'm being harsh, you could check with the client who found his body—he seemed as unconcerned by Mr Hough's death as his neighbours were. A thin, jittery and softly spoken young man, he told the constable everything he knew in a dispassionate and polite manner, all while paying me the utmost respect. Afterwards he thanked the officer for not detaining him and then departed, taking the half-finished coffin Mr Hough had been building for him. Oh, there was something else—my mind is running away from me with all these stories. He also took a golden-brown pelt that had apparently been clutched by what was left of Mr Hough's fingers.

But enough of Thurston Hough! He is as unpleasant in death as he was in life. I believe the time has come to delve into one of my most significant triumphs: my back-to-back victories in the annual Avoca cake-decorating contest, thanks to my secret lavender-icing recipe that doesn't actually contain any lavender—it's just sugar, butter, purple food colouring and marijuana that Larry grows in his backyard.

# GRASS

He had seen many things that filled him with quiet wonder, down at the end of the world. Sky-blanking ice storms, blown up from Antarctica, pelting hail hard enough to scar volcanic rock. Lightning fires that scorched and regenerated the great buttongrass plains. The misting spray of whales; the bulleting breaches of Oneblood tuna; the swishing luminescence of the southern lights, painting the winter nights loud. He saw it all, all that was small and huge and wild and strange, all down there in his far-flung place of work.

He'd been the ranger in the Southwest National Park for ten years. Before that he'd been a junior ranger idling around the mild white-sand reserves of the east coast. Before that he'd been an apprentice carpenter, before that a woodsy teenager, and before that a quiet child, hair constantly strewn with leaves and fingernails thick with dark soil. After school his mother would welcome him home by locking him outside, where their cottage bordered a great forest of eucalyptus and sassafras. She'd press a handful of dry Nutri-Grain into his palm, nudge him towards the trees and go back inside. To many this might seem cruel or selfish, but to the child-ranger it was a gift: a licence to throw himself into a world that was forbidden to others. For two and a half hours every afternoon he'd climb trees, follow tracks, build shelters and swim through the dense green, always feeling a buzz of belonging in his throat and chest. His mother would unlock the back door at dinnertime.

But none of these buzzing, forested afternoons—nor his time later in the gentle east—prepared him for life in the southwest. In his decade there he'd become used to the sights, the storms and beasts and sounds and power, and the waves of wonder that they washed through him—although the first few times it happened, he had been unsettled. He was there to stop poachers, maintain trails, preserve the environment, not to be bowled over by the bright, harsh beauty of his surrounds. Yet soon this bowling over became such a common occurrence that he began to accept it, and once he accepted it he allowed himself to enjoy it: to let the wonder take his soul places it hadn't been since he was a child in the forest, crouching in a branch-built shelter, thirsty for the taste of all the wild things in the world.

The wonder became a regular part of his days. Watching

a seal dance away from a pod of hunting orcas affected him differently to seeing the sky flash purple and iridescent—but he always felt comfortable, appreciative. The wonder was always welcome, and because he welcomed it he'd forgotten it could shock him. It could move him, pause him, shake him, but never with rage or violence. Not until he saw a woman leaking fire at Melaleuca.

Δ

They had come to his hut in the morning, the two young women, and at first he hadn't believed them. They were speaking fast about Allen, how he'd gone mad. Cruel. Wrong. The deaths of the wombats—deaths the ranger hadn't known anything about—had fouled up the man's mind, and now the farmhands were afraid. They wanted to leave, and they wanted the ranger's help to do it.

But as far as he knew, Allen was fine. A quiet man, but a sane one. A good farmer. A friend, or the closest thing to a friend he had down here. So he didn't give these women what they wanted, not straight away. He told them he'd visit the farm. He would see it all for himself, and he would sort things out.

He walked through the frost and wind to find Allen. An hour later he called the parks office and requested a plane for the farmhands.

At dusk, as he watched the plane descend, he reached out and tried to feel the wonder. The wings were shuddering in the wind as the sun, yellow and huge, dropped into an orange horizon. Behind it there was nothing but whipped clouds and glinting water. The world was wild and lonesome, and all of this should have been enough to trigger the wonder—but he couldn't feel it. What he'd seen at the farm was replaying in his mind, blocking everything else. The wombat corpses, lying in the field. The thronging cormorants and their flashing bills, streaked with cold blood. Allen's shouts and threats and red-rimmed eyes. His haggard face. His froth of madness.

The closest thing the ranger had to a friend.

Along with the plane he had called for a doctor, but they wouldn't be able to send one for perhaps a week. He'd have to leave Allen alone until then. There were plenty of things to do: trails to check, supplies to restock, data to gather, but each night he would have to return to his hut, a short walk from Allen and the farm. It would be a week of tension and sorrow. He thought about writing his mother a letter—something he didn't often do, even though he still loved her as fiercely as he had when a child—but the thought petered out as he realised he didn't know what he would say to her. It was all too strange, too unpleasant. He didn't want to burden her with harsh stories.

The plane landed, skidding in a jagged path across the airstrip as the wind refused to release it. The buttongrass was blown flat. The plane could not return now, not in this wind. The pilot would have to stay in one of the bushwalking huts, like the farmhands, and leave in the morning.

The ranger walked to the plane, trying to focus on

the hard wind, the clear sky, the things he loved and found wondrous.

Δ

Something flashed in his dreams, something bright and vivid and real. He woke up. In the darkness he pulled aside the thick curtains in front of his window. All he could see was grass and snow and the small huddled huts. Maybe he hadn't seen anything. Maybe there had been a stray fork of lightning in the sky; maybe the night was fooling him; maybe his fears were planting colours in his head.

But as he was drawing the curtain he saw the blink of a light—something blue, flickering near the farm. He felt his guts drop, and he fumbled for his boots. When he lurched out into the night, with a thrum of fear flicking through him, it was gone. The wind blew and bit. He shoved his hands into his pockets and stumbled off his porch towards the border of the farm, waiting for the light to blink again, but it didn't. All he could see was the farmhouse, and the fields, and the lapping shore of the harbour. And the stars: above him they were as hard and sharp as ever. For a moment he stared up at them, at their harsh, pure light, and tried to convince himself that everything was okay. That he would soon be back in his bed, and he would wake peacefully in the new dawn.

Then he heard the noise: the staccato thumping of boots. The fear thrummed again, and he stared up at the hill closest to the farm. Two figures were running down it: the farm-hands. He began moving towards them, instinct and curiosity pushing him forward, but after a few steps he was stopped by the next thing he saw: the blue light. It wasn't a torch or a siren or cornflower lightning, or any other source of light he'd imagined. It was fire.

Blue flames licked over the top of the hill, steaming the dew from the grass and rushing into the stalks. The flames were low, but they roared down the hill at a tremendous pace, and they were leaving nothing unburnt. The farmhands kept running, and the ranger hung back on the gravel, stupefied. He had to do something, but he didn't know what. Thoughts of fire hoses, of the small extinguisher in his cabin, of rowing out into the harbour all thrashed through his mind, but it wasn't until he heard a shout and a bang from behind him that he remembered: they had a plane.

The shout had come from the pilot, who must have been woken by the noise of the fire, and the bang had come from him yanking the plane's door open. He yelled something at the ranger, waving an arm towards the runway. The ranger turned to the farmhands, who were now less than fifty metres away. He began shouting and motioning towards the plane. They had slowed down, and their strides were heavy, uneven, but when they saw him they changed tack and picked up speed, sprinting for the plane. He ran now too, beating them there by a few lengths.

As they stumbled towards the stairs the pilot started the engine. Its ticking bellow swamped the ranger's ears, just as he started telling them to keep moving, to board the plane, because the farmhands weren't climbing up. The short, red-haired one—her name was Nicola, the ranger remembered—was talking to the taller one, Charlotte, who looked shaken. Her eyes were wide and unfocused, her hands wobbling by her sides. The ranger began exhorting them again; but then he was stopped. Not by Nicola or Charlotte, nor by the pilot or the approaching flames—by what he saw next.

A thin trail of blue tears, the same hue as the fire on the hill, was falling from Charlotte's eyes. The ranger thought she was burning, that sparks had caught in her hair, but then he realised, both understanding completely and not understanding at all: the tears were flames, and they were coming from within Charlotte.

As a fat globule of blueberry fire welled from Charlotte's right eye, Nicola reached out and touched her cheek. The ranger was sure she would be burnt, but at the touch of skin on skin the drop of fire fizzled out. All the other flaming tears stopped, too. Charlotte shook her head, as if coming out of a trance. Nobody spoke. The engine sputtered and groaned.

The flames in the distance were getting closer, and the ranger heard the pilot yelling at them, and finally heeding his urges the farmhands launched themselves into the cabin. One turned back to help the ranger through the door, and together they slammed it shut and shouted for the pilot to take off.

The plane rose as smoke ripped up from the fields. The ranger watched as the farm burned blue, fast and fierce, and the flames tore across the plains.

The pilot asked questions that nobody answered. A field of stars pocked the sky. The flight was dark, but short. The small farmhand kept her hand on the taller one's wrist the whole way.

Δ

The sun rose as the plane fell, diving to scrape its wheels across the tarmac. A pale capital dawn. The ranger promised to explain everything to the pilot, to make sure he was paid overtime, double time, stress pay, whatever he wanted, but he needed to speak to his superiors first. *Come with me*, he told the farmhands. *Everything's going to be all right.*

The tall one looked like she might bolt, but the short one pulled her along, fingers still gripped on a pale wrist. In the reception area of the airport police office he motioned at a few stiff chairs: *Wait here. I'll sort it all out.* He turned to hit the domed silver bell on the desk and waited for someone to appear, a figure of authority he could tell about the fire so that word would spread among the police, the fire service, the rescue patrol, his own department, anyone who needed to know. He'd sit with the farmhands as they were interviewed. If they didn't want to talk about where the flames had come from, he wouldn't say. He hadn't wanted to see what he'd seen, didn't want to know what he knew. They could make something up about campfires or faulty flare guns, and he'd nod and keep his lips shut.

Nobody came to answer his tapping of the bell. He turned to the farmhands, shoulders shrugging, air pushing from his mouth in exasperation. He looked around the small room. He checked the toilet, called their names, pushed his head out the door towards the terminal, but he couldn't find them, and even as he looked he knew he wasn't going to.

He heard the sound of a throat being cleared. A policeman was standing at the desk, looking harassed. The ranger tried to smile, and he tried to come up with something to say. But the disappearance of the farmhands had dragged the weight of concern away with them. He didn't need to tell anyone about what he'd seen. Who would believe him, anyway? And who would it help? He was just a ranger, there to report a fire and make sure the pilot was paid.

That's all he needed to be. That's all he needed to do.

As he walked back towards the desk, fumbling for the right phrases, he was thinking of what Melaleuca would look like now. How the fire, having razed the vegetation, would have burned itself out on the rocky shores of Bathurst Harbour. How the charred humps of buttongrass would already be gleaming with morning dew, hours after burning to their roots. How new shoots would soon spring forth, green and vital, stronger than before. How these bright blades would summon wallabies and potoroos, and with them would come wild wombats, down from the chalky mountains, which would reinforce any survivors from the farm. Birds would follow, too, in the coming months of spring. Orange-bellied parrots, bright and loud in the greenery, and seabirds of all kinds, gulls and sandpipers and oystercatchers, wheeling low among the loose clouds. Whales would slide along the coast, spraying their life-breath high, smacking the dark water white.

He would write to his mother about it, telling her what he was seeing, how he was living every day amid it all. As she read his words she would look out the kitchen window at her own forest, seeing in the swaying trees the origin of the man he had become, the things that had grown and nourished him.

Everywhere the world would open up to him as it used to, huge and humbling; he would be dwarfed by its colour and power. He would forget the farmhands and the fire. In the shudder of his skin, in the run of his blood, he would feel the wonder again.

# SNOW

A memory, sharp as snapped glass: her father coming home on a summer evening. The folds in his face were lined with salt, cooked to a dense crust by the sun through a long day on the water, and his legs were stumping slowly up the driveway—stiff and heavy, knackered. Yet when he looked up to see her waiting behind the rails of their deck his stride lengthened, his knees lifted higher and the salt crust on his face was cracked open by a spreading, full-toothed smile. Their eyes would lock, and the smile would remain in place all the way up the drive, whether it was a good day or bad, right until his scarred hand plunged into her mass of copper ringlets and mixed them into a maze of knots. And even though there was never much else—no hugs, no deep talks, no dancing together at a cousin's wedding—it didn't matter, because it was always enough: the smile that cracked the salt. Even thinking about it now, years later, it still bloomed in her a warmth she could not control or describe, for she knew: she caused that summer smile. She stretched out those tired strides. She split the face he showed the world, and drew his love towards her.

Nothing could conjure the same feeling. Not the apprehensive giddiness of unwrapping a birthday gift, not success at school, not the dizzy red swirl of high-school crushes. Nothing could match the blaze of love in her father's smile. Nothing, that is, until the burn that spread from her stomach the first time she touched Charlotte McAllister.

Δ

She'd grabbed her without thinking. The flames were spreading across the field; they needed to run, but Charlotte wasn't moving; she was just pushing out heavy breaths, staring at Allen's fleeing figure while she continued to leak her flames. Nicola grabbed her. That's all it was—a thoughtless lunge, fingers wrapping a wrist—and in that moment of contact she felt it: the burn. Through her throbbing fingertips she could feel the source of the flame, pulsing out from deep inside Charlotte. Then she felt it waver, slow, and die, and in that instant she knew: she had done this. Her touch had travelled through Charlotte's heat. She had quenched the rage; she had stopped the fire.

Charlotte's face went slack. They saw the flames on the

ground, how they were spreading and growing, and then they were running, flying, numbing, landing and soon sitting in that airport office. As the ranger turned his back Nicola was thinking only of the police, what they might do, how she'd explain it, how crazy it all sounded. She thought Charlotte was too exhausted to talk; she hadn't said a word since the fire. But as Nicola's thoughts turned to Allen and his madness, she felt a hand shaking her knee. Charlotte was flicking her eyes between Nicola and the door: *let's go.*

And Nicola—who was always so measured, so thoughtful, so full of plans and logic and duty—was standing up and following her. Quiet feet touched grey carpet. The latch clicked shut. In moments they had made it to the other side of the airport, to the long-term car park where Nicola had left the old station wagon her parents had lent her. The key twisted: once in the door, again in the ignition. A cold engine ticked into life. Tyres bit and rolled. And before they could be stopped, before a calm and clever plan could be teased out, they were on the highway, going north.

Δ

Charlotte slept. Nicola drove, tired enough to feel sick but not to sleep, for she was full of running, leaping thoughts. Thoughts of blue fire and unburnt skin. Of her father's smile; of her fingers on a cold wrist; of different kinds of burns. Of police; of her family; of Allen; of the ranger; of eyeless, blood-painted wombat bodies; of what lay ahead, and what she'd just left.

Thoughts of where they were heading, and where they should hide. Her mind circled and dragged, tripping on memories of places she'd felt safe. Unil she knew where they could go.

Δ

When Allen had brought Charlotte up from the dock Nicola was tired and in desperate need of a friend. She'd known it would be this way—nobody goes to Melaleuca, not in winter—but she'd thought she'd be able to handle it. The work was rewarding, the wombats filled her with joy, and the experience, for someone her age, was impossible to find anywhere else. But she needed human contact beyond quiet conversations with Allen and occasionally the ranger, so when she saw Charlotte get out of the ute she felt a sudden, bursting thrill. A visitor; a companion; maybe even a friend. At the very least, someone to talk to.

Charlotte barely looked at her—not there in the driveway, and not for days afterwards. Even when they were introduced and Nicola found out she'd be staying to work on the farm, Charlotte's eyes would not drift from the ground or sky. It was as if she was trying to blend in with the fields and snow. As she showed Charlotte around the farm Nicola let her eyes linger on her face longer than was polite, trying to provoke her into looking back. Nothing. The thrill Nicola had first felt ebbed away into a small, sharp pebble of disappointment.

Charlotte was good at the work, Nicola soon learned. The wombats took an instinctive liking to her, and she didn't mind the dirt, the cold, the frost. She continued to keep to herself. The evenings in the farmhouse were quiet and dull. It stayed that way for a few weeks, and it probably wouldn't have changed all winter, if not for the deaths and the change that came over Allen.

There was only one good outcome to his increasingly violent mood swings: it brought Nicola and Charlotte closer. At first they just discussed what was happening, but as Allen became more erratic they began spending more time together. The wombats kept dying; the madness in Allen kept growing; and then they were walking everywhere together, making sure each knew where the other was, and soon Charlotte was sleeping on the floor of Nicola's bedroom.

By the night of the fire they were creeping to the edges of a friendship. A friendship defined by shared danger, but a friendship nonetheless. There was too much happening for Nicola to dwell on it, but she could feel it happening: the closing distance between them, the comfort of company, the urge to reach and touch.

Δ

The station wagon rolled on through the Midlands, past farms, fences, gold-grey cylinders of harvested wheat, over barren Spring Hill, past the sandstone of Oatlands and the splatter of Tunbridge, heading north, north, north. An hour later Nicola twisted the wheel left, and they rolled down into the Meander Valley. Stubbled Midlands gave way to the spiderish irrigators and green glow of dairy country. Dolerite tiers rose at the western edge of the flatlands, dark and steep, their jagged columns free of the gum forests that clung to their slopes. The rattling wagon passed the slow South Esk, fields of patchwork cattle, the occasional berry farm, and then swung northwest at the pull of Nicola's arm. Her eyelids were pulling, too; she'd barely slept for two days, but she did not want to stop, not when they were so close.

At Sheffield, her head rocking forward, she parked outside a small supermarket. They had closed in on the great tiers; the closest one glinted with clean snow as it loomed above the town. It was late afternoon. The farmers were still in their fields, schoolchildren had come and gone, and the town was slumped in wintry solitude. She should have slept, if only for a few moments. But Charlotte was still sleeping, and she did not want to wake her. Instead she wandered into the supermarket and bought enough food to last them a month.

On she drove, leaving the highway, up a skinny country road, past the snow-capped tier and into the forest on its foothills. The road twirled into the thickening treescape, dropped into a gorge, passed a rumbling hydro station and rose sharply up the other side of the valley. On this zig-zagging incline Charlotte stirred. Nicola had hit a rock, and the extra pulse of vibration in the window was finally enough to wake her up. She rubbed at her eyes and asked: *Where are we?*

Nicola, yawning. *Nearly there.*

Charlotte shifted in her seat, straightening up, looking around. *Nearly where?* She had fallen asleep amid blunt crops and grey fields, but now she saw a dense, deep dark-green wall of tree ferns, myrtles, moss. Nicola yawned again. *Somewhere safe.*

The car climbed on, and the world was not done morphing. As Nicola piloted them ever upwards the crowded gloom of the ferny forest thinned and was gradually replaced by shorter trees and bigger gaps in the foliage, gaps wide enough to reveal shards of the darkening sky. As they crested the last rise, the green walls disappeared entirely. They had emerged onto a flat plain. Here there were no forests, no ferns, no lushness of leaf or frond or fungus. Stunted snowgums, their twisted trunks a melodic whirl of beige-green-brown, gnarled out of the ground sporadically between the field of lichen-scarred boulders. Flat ponds of standing winter water were scattered among the rocks, along with stubbled bushes and pale deadwood, and everything was smattered with drifts of bright snow. It took them both a few minutes to adjust to this strange, muted landscape. Charlotte was still groggy, and Nicola was exhausted; by the time either of them had thought of anything useful to say Nicola was swinging left again, at the urging of a sign: Cradle Mountain.

Charlotte threw her a glance. *This place is full of tourists.*

Nicola shook her head, as much to keep herself awake as to disagree, and mumbled: *Not all of it.*

Charlotte looked back out the window. They were slowing down now, as black speed humps and yellow wildlife signs began to crowd the road. Small huts and wooden lodges poked out of the thin bush. Car parks and walking trails huddled close to the asphalt, and then they were passing a sprawling visitor centre and a parks office. Charlotte pointed at the sign. *I came here as a kid.*

Nicola, blinking furiously. *Me too.*

From here the black road narrowed further, winding and dipping amid the snow, until Nicola lurched the car into a small car park beside another pond-pocked plain. Before her eyelids could drop she swung her legs out of the car. The highland air bit at her face. She moved to the boot, where she grabbed a coat, beanie and gloves from the emergency bag of clothes her mother, a tourism operator, always kept in the car. Charlotte had gotten out too, her questions hijacked by *shit* and *fuck* and *holy shit, it's fucking freezing* as she joined Nicola to rug up. Nicola grabbed the rest of the clothes, half the groceries, and pointed across the plain. A trail of wooden duckboards led through the snow towards a scraggly forest. *This way. It'll take fifteen minutes.*

Charlotte picked up the rest of the groceries. *Where the hell are we going?*

Nicola let her foot hit the first duckboard. *It won't take long.* Another heavy step. *Please.* She pushed on, not looking to see if Charlotte was following but knowing she was— she could hear her boots landing on the wet wood behind her, a thudding monotone that through her exhaustion still somehow lit the kindling in her gut.

Across the boards they trudged, wind cutting them, snow tripping them, until they reached a rocky path that wound between the whorled trees. Up they went, past a cold mountain stream that gushed between banks of snow. Five minutes later, as Charlotte stumbled over a great boulder and let out a foggy gasp, they found the source of the stream: a slate-grey lake. Its surface held a pattern of tiny waves, roused by the wind, and on every side it was bordered by black cliffs of steeply climbing, sharply crumbling dolerite, covered in patches by snow. Nicola joined her on the boulder, two words escaping between her clattering teeth: *Crater Lake.*

She then lifted an arm towards something Charlotte had not seen: a large hut, built of stone, sitting on the edge of the lake.

Δ

It belonged to a friend of her father's, a fish trader named Oshikawa. He had bought it two decades earlier as a place to escape the ocean. Unlike Nicola's father he had no abiding love for the coast, or the fish, or even his job. He viewed fish meat and saltwater simply as necessities of his career—privately, he preferred the dark mountains in the Central Highlands. At the end of each fishing season he would sell the last of his stock and relocate to the hut for at least a month. Here he would hike the great peaks that scraped the sky in every direction, often staying out for days, only returning to his hut by the lake when he'd run out of food.

He liked it up here so much that he occasionally invited friends to come enjoy it with him: fellow wholesalers, visitors from Japan, and the odd client and their family—like Nicola's father. Nicola had been here a few years earlier, not long after her father's seal died. And now, without Oshikawa's permission, she was back.

Δ

Nicola's plan was simple: to bring Charlotte somewhere fireproof. Up here there were stone walls, and a stone roof, and stone-cold snow in every direction. The vegetation was not thick and it was always wet. Outside their front door was a deep, ice-edged lake. If Charlotte's fire escaped again there would be little for her to destroy, and lots of ways to put out her flames. Here they could rest. Nobody would find them. Summer was months away, and Oshikawa would be too busy to come on a holiday. They could stay as long as they needed to—as long as Charlotte wanted. And once she was sure she had her fire under control, once they were sure she wouldn't burn down any hospitals or playgrounds, they would head back to the capital. They would go to the police, answer their questions and apologise to the ranger. Everything would be okay.

That was it: hide, recover, re-emerge. Nicola hadn't factored herself or her needs into this plan; that wasn't her way. Since her days on the deck, cracking open her father's smile, she had lived by putting others first. Her first instinct was always to help, to shrink back from the front and push others forward. It wasn't pure selflessness; she drew pleasure from how she could affect others, and when they showed her gratitude she bathed in it, glowing in the knowledge that she, and only she, had made them feel that way.

But this plan with Charlotte—this was different. Nicola was being driven by something more powerful than a desire to help, more urgent than a taste for gratitude. Something red and foggy. It knocked, fast and firm, through her veins.

Δ

Inside the hut there were two blanket-covered couches, a sparse bookshelf, an open kitchen adorned with hanging cast-iron frypans, two doors leading off into bedrooms, one into a bathroom, and a huge black wood heater that dominated the eastern wall. The walls were built with stacked slate, held together by some kind of mortar. They seemed impractical, especially for somewhere this remote, but Nicola didn't care; slate would not burn. The floors were wooden and covered by a thick layer of faded rugs, but nothing could be done about that.

The temperature was no higher than outside. Charlotte began gathering twigs and paper from a wicker basket by the fireplace. Nicola watched her, thought about helping, then collapsed on a couch. Sleep swallowed her; she didn't even have time to take off her boots, or watch as Charlotte searched the hut for matches before realisation swam across her face and she returned to the wood heater, peeled off a glove and gingerly shook her wrist until a shower of blue sparks sprayed out from beneath her fingernails onto the dry fuel.

Nicola was woken sometime between two and three in the morning. She opened her eyes, and in the cave-dark hut briefly lost her bearings. She couldn't remember where she was, or how she had gotten there, but then she realised that Charlotte was sleeping on the other couch. Calmness replaced confusion, but only for a moment. Her nostrils zinged, and she realised what had woken her up: smoke.

She turned to the wood heater, expecting embers to have fallen from its mouth, but the door was closed. A blackened log lay on a bed of glowing coals, and no sparks, flames or smoke were leaking from it. Nicola turned back to Charlotte, looking harder through the darkness, and saw a thin blue trail worming out of her ear. It had reached the cushion beside her head—a wispy, plasticky stream of it, rising up into the cabin. As Nicola scrambled towards Charlotte the smoking patch of cushion erupted into a small blue flame. With one hand she smacked it out, and with the other she rested a palm on Charlotte's hot cheek.

Through her palm she again felt the pulse of flame from within Charlotte's body. Again she felt it flicker out. She felt the burn in her stomach, hot and red, and knew she'd doused the fire. Again she didn't want to let go.

The flame died. The fire stopped leaking from Charlotte's ear; her eyes flew open. Confusion appeared on her face, and she raised a sleepy arm to brush away Nicola's hand. Nicola pointed at the burnt cushion. *Sorry. But you were…*

Charlotte looked down at the black mark. Her nose twitched. *Shit.* She rubbed at her ear. *Sorry. I've got to get a handle on this.*

*It's all right*, said Nicola.

Charlotte stopped rubbing her ear and stood up. *No, it's*

*not.* She strode to the basket near the wood heater. *Go back to sleep. I'll stay up.*

Nicola was going to argue, but Charlotte was poking more wood into the fire and paying her no attention. Her eyes were focused on the heater; the conversation was over. Nicola slunk back to her couch and lay down, watching Charlotte tend the coals through half-closed eyes until sleep found her again.

Δ

Hours later, as light crawled into the hut, she woke back up. Charlotte was in the kitchen, unpacking groceries into the small cupboards. A metal kettle was boiling on top of the stove. As Nicola rose from the couch Charlotte brought her a slice of buttered toast.

In the bedrooms they found proper highland jackets— thermal, fleece-lined, waterproof—and with the sky clear of storms, and with nothing else to do, they went out into the winter. Black spurs of the mountain range poked high and sharp above them, daggering up into the pale sky. The sheer cliffs that fell away from these peaks revealed great faces of jagged Jurassic rock. Down where the land was less vertical snowgums gnarled their way out of frozen dirt, their trunks a patchwork of grey-brown-green, as if all the colours of the forest had poured themselves into a single species of tree. Small bushes huddled among these low gums, and between the trees and bushes currawongs flapped, their white tail feathers contrasting against their black plumage and yolk-yellow eyes.

Charlotte started walking. Nicola followed. The track they'd taken the day before continued past the hut and around the southern edge of Crater Lake, carved into the cliff. Through the trees and over the boulders they walked, stopping every now and then to catch their breath and stare over at the cliffs and lake. Other than to warn each other about head-high branches and slippery rocks they did not speak—even though Nicola wanted to talk to Charlotte, she felt no words rise up in her. The track steepened, and after an uneasy climb they found themselves on the edge of the crater that gave its name to the lake. Now they could see beyond the cliffs, over to dozens more mountains, lakes, the road they'd followed the day before, and beyond it the great wide plain of the highland plateau. The road ended at a car park near another, bigger lake. Tiny dots of tourists were anting around its edge on a wide, flat path.

And above all this, right in from of them: the twin peaks of Cradle Mountain, joined by a sagging, rough dent. White and black, high and low, harsh in its peaks and welcoming in its sling: a sight reserved for postcards, and galleries. They walked on, scaling a few more lookouts, where the air was even colder and the snow was shin deep and even the snowgums could not grow. They did not attempt to climb Cradle—they didn't have the supplies or the gear, or any need to try something so daunting. They avoided the tourists at the lake, sticking to paths that circled icy tarns, before they agreed that it was getting late and they needed to eat something.

On the trudge back Charlotte asked: *So what's the plan?*

Nicola's first, automatic thoughts: hands wrapping, skin touching. But she swept those aside, and started mumbling out her plan: how as soon as Charlotte had gotten control of her… *episodes*, she called them…they would go back and sort everything out with the police and the ranger and whoever else.

*I thought they might lock you up or something*, she said.

Charlotte said: *Yeah. Well.* She pulled her jacket around her throat. *What if I can't?* She kicked a rock off a ledge. *Control it.*

Nicola didn't know what to say.

They descended on the track they'd taken earlier in the day, the lake and cliffs and hut all opening up before them. Nicola felt anxious, worried that Charlotte thought the plan was stupid, that she was stupid, but when they were inside the hut she showed no sign of it. She threw some old paper and kindling into the wood heater and lit it by hacking some sticky blue phlegm out of her throat. Nicola was fumbling around with the groceries, but Charlotte took over that, too, chopping and dicing and boiling for half an hour until two bowls of something like spaghetti marinara sat on their laps in front of the fire. After Charlotte ate, she had a shower and went to bed.

Nicola did both these things too, straight after Charlotte. It took her a long time to get to sleep.

Δ

The smoke found her nose sometime in the deep, ink-lined morning. She lurched up and out and into Charlotte's room, where a small forest of blue flames was pouncing out of her toenails and feasting on the sheet at the end of her bed. Nicola ran forward and grabbed her ankles.

Hot touch. Wild flicker. Cold fade.

The fire stopped falling from Charlotte's feet, but the established flames still burned, lapping at the skin on Nicola's wrists. Charlotte woke up, shouted, swore, kicked off Nicola's hands and leaped forward onto the flames. She smacked them out with hard hands, impervious to the heat.

Afterwards she sat on the end of the bed, breathing heavily. Nicola held her wrists for a moment, then shuffled into the kitchen to run them under water. The burns weren't bad. They'd heal in a day or two. Charlotte appeared behind her, swearing and apologising. *It's okay*, Nicola mumbled. *I'm fine.* She lifted her wrists to show her, and through the darkness Charlotte could see the shiny patch of burn, and she swore even louder.

Nicola followed her back into her room, where Charlotte was crouching on the bed, knees held up to her chin. *It's all right, it's really all right*, she said, but Charlotte kept muttering *fuck, fuck, shit, fuck.*

*Maybe I should stay in here.* Charlotte looked up at her. Nicola's throat cinched, her wrists stung, as she said: *You stop doing it when I touch you.*

Charlotte turned away from her. *No.* She kicked her legs back under the doona. *Look at your arms.*

*I'm fine*, said Nicola, with no conviction. She turned to leave the room.

*Wait.* She turned again: Charlotte had pulled the covers back on the other side of the bed. *All right.*

△

There were no more fires that night. None the following night, either, nor the third. Charlotte slept peacefully, lying on her side facing the wall, while Nicola lay on her back trying not to look at or touch her. During the mornings they walked along the trails, seeking out new waterfalls, peaks, tarns, fields of snow and heather. In the afternoons Charlotte would sit by the lake or in front of the wood heater, making odd noises with her throat and nose, and strange movements with her feet and ears. At first Nicola thought she might have gone mad, but then she realised Charlotte was trying to summon her flames. Trying to control them.

It was hard to tell if it was working. Sometimes she could click her fingers and a perfect lick of fire would snap out of her thumbnail, like a fleshy Zippo lighter. Other times she would hack and cough for hours with no results, only to get the hiccups later on and accidentally spit fire all over her lap. Her pants had fibrous, brown-shined burn marks. It was a vague sign of progress, if not control.

While this was going on Nicola lounged in front of the wood heater, reading her way through Oshikawa's bookshelf. Other times she cooked—she was not as good as Charlotte, but she could bake scones, simmer sauce, sauté onions and potatoes. In the evenings they'd eat, wash up, play cards or attempt the board games and puzzles that Oshikawa had left stacked under the bookshelf. When they spoke about what had happened in Melaleuca they did so in broad terms, with relief and anger—Nicola saying *At least most of the wombats would have survived* and Charlotte saying *I hope Allen didn't.* When they spoke about their families Nicola would give gentle, general descriptions of her mother and sister, along with shorter pictures of her father, his salted smile, how he'd become wrecked and hollow after the orcas took his seal. Charlotte wouldn't say much at all, other than that her mother was dead, her brother was hard to deal with and her father had never known how to be a father. Then the conversation would falter, and they'd focus again on the cards or board game, until the fire burned low and they went to bed.

They'd change in separate rooms, climb in each side of the shared bed and say goodnight. Charlotte, breathing deeply, would always fall asleep first.

Δ

The next fire happened a week after they had arrived. Nicola was awake this time, staring up at the ceiling. Charlotte mumbled and turned onto her back, which drew Nicola's attention, just as a rivulet of flames began leaking out of the side of her mouth. Without thinking Nicola leaned over and placed a hand on Charlotte's chin. The fire didn't stop, so she ran her hand down Charlotte's neck, then back up the chin towards the flames, searching for the flicker within her body. Charlotte's eyes opened. She sucked the fire back into her mouth.

*Do that again.*

Nicola withdrew her hand. *Sorry—your mouth. I...*

Charlotte sat up. *I know.* Her hand found Nicola's, pulling it towards her. *Do it again.*

Δ

In the morning they slept in. Nicola was the first to wake. Just like their first night at the hut she was confused about where she was, but then she remembered. Charlotte's body was bumped against her own. Their knees were locked together. A stiff muscle in her back prompted Nicola to roll over, and she tried gently to disentangle herself, which woke Charlotte up. Without speaking she reached one hand behind Nicola's neck, dancing her fingers into her curls. Her other hand slid over Nicola's side to grasp her thigh, a hard, pulling grasp, and then her mouth was on Nicola's neck, and Nicola had somehow made it onto her back, just like she'd been trying to.

Eventually they did get up—Charlotte first, walking naked through the hut to stoke the wood heater, while Nicola tried to pull on her clothes and stared at Charlotte's jutting angles and morning skin. They cooked toast over the fire, ate slowly, got dressed, and wandered outside as they usually did without talking about what had happened, though as they went out the door Charlotte rested a small hand on Nicola's back, and Nicola, without thinking, pulled her in by her jacket and kissed her. Their teeth knocked, hard and cold.

They did a short lap of Crater Lake and ended up sitting on a rock overlooking the small forest and duckboard trail that led down to the road. The air, already cold, was taking on an icier edge around them. They should go inside, Nicola thought, but her fingers were interlocked with Charlotte's, and their heads were gently bumping together, and she did not want to move.

Charlotte lifted her free arm and said: *Look*.

Nicola followed the line of her arm. In the little gravel car park, next to the station wagon, was a car. It was too far away for Nicola to make out any of its features, other than that it was white. On the duckboards, bent into the mountain wind, was a person trudging towards them. Police, Nicola thought, or the ranger, or even Oshikawa, coming to check on his property in the middle of the tuna season. She felt Charlotte stiffen. *It's probably just a tourist*, Nicola said. But she did not believe it.

Neither of them moved. Soon they could see that the stranger was wearing a long grey overcoat. A city coat, nothing like the thermal jackets people wear in the highlands. The figure reached the treeline and disappeared, following the path as it wound past the stream and waterfall.

Nicola shivered. It could just be a daytripper, wandering along the wrong path. But if it was someone who'd come to find them, she didn't want to meet them. Her skin was chilled but her veins had never been hotter; Charlotte's hand was resting on her knee, and she didn't want all this taken away from her. She wanted it with an intensity that she couldn't remember feeling before: a white-churned feeling of fear and sorrow and urgency.

For so long she had been putting others first. Now, with this taste of want on her tongue, she surged with thoughts of herself. Hard desires. Sharp needs.

Charlotte was staring at the trees that the stranger had entered.

Ten more minutes passed, ten minutes of shivering in the wind with the grey dish of Crater Lake and the black walls of the mountain behind them. Snow was falling now. They needed to go inside. The stranger, so poorly coated, might not make it through the trees in this weather.

But then, stomping onto the trail that led out of the trees was a pair of worn black boots. Rising from the boots were legs wrapped in old jeans, and above them a thin shirt. Around this shirt was the long coat they'd identified earlier, pulled tight with gloveless blue-white hands. And out of this set of ill-chosen clothes poked the neck and head of a woman. Short, slick hair. Cherry lips. Hard eyes, yet the lines around their corners leaked out a sense of relief when she straightened up and saw them waiting on the rock.

At the edge of the trees, ten metres from where they sat, she stopped trudging. Charlotte stood up. The woman put her hands into the small of her back and stretched, before wrapping her arms around herself and shivering under the soft-falling snow.

*You girls got any gin?*

# WOOD

Levi is retching. He is standing in a small house, surrounded by a cloud of foul, rot-filled air. A corpse lies at his feet. Almost all of the exposed skin and flesh on the body has been ripped or chewed off, but Levi knows who it is: Thurston Hough. It must be. This is the address Hough's publisher gave him. If the face was whole Levi would recognise it from the author photo in his copy of *The Wooden Jacket*, but a grey-red mess of stale meat, thick with flies and greenish slime, sits where eyes and ears, cheeks and lips should be. The rest of the body is clothed in khaki trousers and a flannelette shirt, except for the feet and fingers, which are as mutilated as the face. The smell is unbearable: a blanket of sour, rancid heat. White bone and yellow teeth glint up at him from the bloody wreckage.

Levi retches again, feeling bitter bile gush up his throat and out onto the dusty floor.

Levi is leaning on his knees, trying to breathe through his mouth, when he sees the pelt clutched in the skeletal fingers of Hough's right hand. It is a rich shade of golden-brown, and is clenched tightly in the dead grip, as if the last of Hough's energy went into holding onto it. It takes Levi a few seconds to peel back the stiff bones and release it. When it comes free it slides snugly into his palm, warm and plush, and suddenly he no longer feels ill. The stench becomes bearable; the horrifying corpse becomes mundane.

Levi is filled with confidence and a renewed sense of purpose. His veins are buzzing; he is striding past the body now, forgetting Hough, clutching the fur and searching for the coffin he knows must be there, the coffin he had commissioned. He finds it, half-finished—polished and square at one end, hollow and sawdust-strewn at the other—in a creaky workshop behind the house.

Levi is driving. The highway is snaking along the South Esk, pushing west, away from the slow streets of Avoca, and he doesn't plan on going back there ever again, not unless someone puts a knife to his throat. The cop he'd spoken to about the body had been so ponderous, so kind, and Levi had no time for his meandering questions and glacial train of thought. Even worse had been the attentions of the old woman who had pestered him from the moment he entered the town, touching his back, offering him scones, nattering inane comments with every huffing breath. It feels good to be out of there, to have Hough dead and gone and forgotten, to have Avoca slammed permanently in his past. The half-finished coffin is rattling on the tray of his ute.

Levi is stroking the pelt as he pushes his foot further down, taking the corners too quick; he's lucky the road is dry and the traffic is thin. The prized fur is warm and lush beneath his fingers, and this heat is travelling up through his hand and into his head, his lungs, his stomach. He is beginning to understand why Hough kept ranting about it in his letters. The richness of its touch is shaving the edges off his anger, giving him room to think, and at the forefront of his thoughts is the snowgum coffin he is hauling. The coffin that is incomplete.

Levi is leaving the eastern valleys and turning out onto the Midlands Highway, thinking: I'm going to have to finish it myself. But he has no skills of craftsmanship or wood-working. He has no friends with those skills (he has no friends at all, not in the true, call-each-other-for-no-reason sense); he knows no builders, no cabinetmakers, and besides, he is running out of the money his mother left him.

Levi is reminding himself of his resolve: to show Charlotte that she wasn't condemned to rise again, changed and ghastly, after she died. That her life needn't end twice. That she needn't suffer the same fate as their mother. That he had sourced this calming coffin for her and her alone; that in the face of their sorrow he had gone to great lengths to have it built; that he couldn't go another day knowing she was in such pain; that he cared for her this much; that he loved her more than he could ever show with words; that the coffin represented all this.

Levi is not well. Levi is not realising: he could have just spoken to her. In a mind like his, grand acts will always trump honest words. There was a chance he'd understand this—a slim chance, but a chance nonetheless—the moment he saw the coffin. An epiphany might have dawned upon him: What am I doing? Is she even worried about her eventual death? What if she just needs someone to talk to? What if she just needs time? But this chance was destroyed the moment Levi picked the golden-brown pelt from Hough's nibbled fingers. Now, with his fingers tousling the fur, with the uncommon warmth spreading from his fingers to his scalp, he has never been more sure of himself.

Levi is not safe. Levi is hurtling north, past the muddy fields and sad-eyed sheep of the lowlands, telling himself: Yes. I will finish the coffin. How hard can it be? It only takes tools, wood, nails and varnish—he can source these without too much trouble. Snowgums are plentiful in the high hills in the north of the island. He will find one out on the moors, chop it down, heave it onto the ute, haul it home and saw it into planks. He is a man; he is capable; he can do this.

Levi is skirting the docklands of Launceston, bumping over a bridge at the mouth of the South Esk, above the silt and eels and past the gaping gorge, and rolling on into the Tamar Valley. The light is dimming into a yellow smudge on the horizon. The broad salty river is blinking points of bright-white-deep-blue up at him, and he is forced to lift a hand to his eyes. He fumbles in the glovebox, eventually retrieving a pair of black sunglasses. They belonged to his father. He would wear them whenever he drove, regardless of the weather, and Levi always found this suspicious. It *was* suspicious: it could be pouring with rain or the valley could've been swamped with fog, but as soon as he got in the car his father would slide these sunglasses on, as if they were as necessary as a seatbelt.

Levi is pushing the arms of the glasses behind his ears, and as the cool plastic rests on his skin he wonders: Will he be home? At this time of day? The ute is rattling past the bakery town of Exeter. The old man's wooden mansion is only five minutes away. His father's face bounces into his mind. The fur burns in his fingers, and then he is pulling the sunglasses off and throwing them back into the glovebox. He blinks at the dying light. The fur burns again, and the image of his father's face is shaded dark red. Another image appears: the rubbing fronds and rising flames of his mother's second death, and now Levi is bruising past the turnoff at a dangerous pace.

Levi is pushing straight on into the dips and humps of the green valley, rising and falling with the heave of the land, his unshielded eyes blinded by the sun bouncing off the salt river, driving on memory alone. After twenty minutes he crests the final hill and drops down to the little farm. He parks beside the cottage and goes inside, where there isn't much light and even less warmth, but there is, among the dusty shelves and boot-worn floorboards, the unmistakable pillowy feeling of coming home. Even in the midst of his rock-hard resolve, Levi cannot dodge this feeling. It reaches out at him from the faded floral curtains. It snags him from the sagging bookshelves. It rises through the chipped tiles behind the old stove. Through the windows of the front lounge he can see the dark ocean heaving against the rocky coast, and that, too, splashes him with this coming-home comfort. The waves are breaking white. The sun has fifteen, maybe twenty minutes left.

Levi is striding through the thistled fields towards a lonely beach. It lies at the edge of their lowest gully, between two tall walls of red-grey rock. It's the only stretch of sand on their property. It's where he and Charlotte would come every day of summer, running through the heat to swim and shout, although she did most of the shouting and all of the swimming. It's where his mother would sit quietly at the end of most days. It's where his father would not come, not past the gully edge, for he was afraid of the ocean. It's where Levi has now arrived, out of breath and slightly dizzy, thinking of Charlotte and the water. She's all he's thought about for weeks. That's what's brought him here: memories of her, and the joy she'd take in those first cold leaps into the deep. Her flinging, shrieking, whirring presence, always vibrating in his peripheries. Always redefining what their father called a *commotion*. Always urging him to join in.

Levi is remembering, as these memories lap at his mind: Charlotte is missing. He has been telling himself that she will come back when she's ready, that she is safe, that she can look after herself. He's been saying it for so long that these thoughts have become reflexive. But the sun is dropping, the sea is cracking, the memories are lap, lap, lapping, and here on the beach his resolve is beginning to waver. Charlotte could be anywhere, with anyone. She could be sick. She could be dead. She could be fine, but she could have decided to never return. Levi's breathing has shallowed out. Bile tangs at his tongue. And as the dusk lies down and dread begins gnawing, he is remembering something else: he left the pelt in the house.

Levi is marching up through the fields, missing steps, growing cold. A light is on in the house; he does not remember leaving one on. Adrenaline stills his shivering arms as he pushes through the door, and for a few moments he forgets about the pelt. Into the house he goes, where it is warmer than it should be. He treads down the hall. The kettle is boiling in the kitchen, a fire is snapping in the lounge, and between these points of heat is their source: his father, sitting at the dining table.

Levi is staring. His father does not look up. *Hello, Levi.*

Levi is spitting. *What are you doing here?*

His father is standing up. *Saying hello. Where's your sister? Not here.*

His father is tossing a pinecone into the fire. *I know that. I thought you might have spoken to her.*

Levi is trying to stop anger and confusion and other, murkier feelings from chopping his words into harsh little yips as he mutters: *I haven't.*

His father is watching the flames lick and rise. *I know*

*things have been…difficult. But you need to—I don't know. Clear your head.*

Levi is refusing to abandon his manners, even as he wants to roar and curse. *Please leave.*

His father is turning to face him. *You're not healthy, son. Ever since your mother died…*

*I asked you to leave.*

His father is moving now, coming towards him. *You're not yourself.*

*You need to leave, before I call the police.*

His father is still walking, slow and sure, saying: *Your sister will come home, eventually, and you need to be reliable. Strong. The brother you normally are.*

Levi is feeling his resolve splinter against his desire to scream and scream, but he stays quiet, because amid his hammering thoughts he has suddenly remembered why he returned from the beach. He walks over to the bench and grabs the pelt. His fingers dive into its thick fibres; heat surges through his arm; his resolve takes back its hardness. Levi takes a deep breath. He looks at his father—right into his ever-shifting eyes—and says: *I haven't seen you since the cremation.*

His father stops. *Levi…*

Levi is talking in a louder voice now, louder and more purposeful. *The last time I saw you before that was over a year ago.*

His father rubs his eyes. *I know. Listen…*

Levi is barking. *No.*

His father is exhaling slowly and saying: *There are reasons. Not good ones. But your mother—*

Levi is shouting: *Get out!* His free palm is slamming onto the bench.

His father is rubbing at his scalp. He is saying: *I'm sorry. I'm so sorry. You know what I'm like…*

*No, I don't.*

*Please. Just try to—*

Levi isn't listening, because if his father won't leave, Levi will. He is striding outside into the heatless arms of the farm, where in the clean black night he is not cold. A fire is crackling through him. The pelt is in his hand. His father is not following him, and Levi does not care if he does, because he does not care about the man, not about who he is or what he says or where he goes, because at the mention of his mother he has stopped caring about almost everything: he has realised what he needs to do.

Levi is wandering over to the ute. He peers into the tray at the half-finished coffin. The grey snowgum planks are splashed with the twirling patterns of the highlands. They will take his sister's body and turn it cold and hard as dolerite, forever preserved beneath the soil, and they are not right; they will not do; they aren't what Charlotte needs. No—her wooden jacket will be crafted out of something much more personal. And he will build it himself.

# COAL

He was born in the instant a woman, crouching by the curl of a cold river, smacked two smooth stones together. From that crash of rock flew a spark, and in that spark there was heat, light…and him. Somewhere inside that tiny flick of fire he began to exist, first as a hot thought, then as a proto-mind. There were no words or emotions; there was just life. His life. All he knew was that he existed, that he burned and that he was falling.

But he was lucky: the spark fell not onto wet dirt or frosted meadow but into a cradle of dry leaves that the woman had prepared. He smouldered, bright and impotent, until he followed an instinctive urge to suck himself into the dead vegetation. Here, in a hot spurt of physicality, he began to glow. The grass blackened, pale smoke plumed and in a bursting lick of brightness, he was not a spark but a flame, a tongue of yellow-orange fire that grew and danced and rose, chewing up the leaf nest and spitting out black char.

As the flame expanded, so did his mind. A greater depth of thought blew out of him—thoughts with edges, curves and the early spikes of emotion—as well as an expanded field of orange-tinged vision. He began to see that around him there was dead fuel, yes, but there was also sharp life. Gold-black bees tumbled through the green grass beyond his reach. White specks of birds hung against the blue dome above him. Yabbies clicked on the riverbank. And the most obvious and important life in his new world was now feeding him, her creased brown fingers poking dry sticks into his dancing maw, causing him to sputter, fizzle and grow even taller.

Under her tender ministrations he leaped upwards, taking on new colours and shapes, learning the distinctive tastes of twig and branch and grass without ever feeling satisfied—his hunger, he discovered, was without end. But as much as he wanted to feast, he wanted even more to please his creator. With his hungry yellow tongues he helped her harden a branch, shaping its end into a charred point. He took a wallaby she dropped in his coals and singed off its fur, melted its tendons and burned its flesh. He spat ash into her palms, which she mixed with water and applied to her face in a slick slurry. And as he did all this he realised he had a purpose; that she had called him into life for a specific set of reasons; that he could do so much more than eat and grow.

And then his mother taught him fear. Without warning she gathered scoops of water from the river and splashed out his eyes, his tongues, his limbs, and as he sizzled under the drenching wetness he learned a new taste: horror. In a swift moment he changed from a crackling god into a blinking, dying ember, spewing out his final breaths in a thin strand of smoke. The woman stood up, gathered her possessions, and walked away. His mind had turned woozy and weak. From his little coal he couldn't see much more than clumps of wet grey ash, and beyond them her naked retreating feet. In such a short time he had lived, learned, grown and died. A cold wind streaked across his face. The ember glowed hard, bright, and out.

Δ

But he did not die; he merely slept. Sometime later—hours, days, weeks—a crooked stick of lightning lanced a dead paperbark at the back of a white beach. There was an explosion of woodchips, sparks, fire, and in the midst of all this mayhem his mind roared back to consciousness. He surged up through the flames, looking around, feeding on the paperbark, and saw that his mother and the river were gone. Instead he was surrounded by a scraggly forest, gritty sand, great orange rocks, and beyond all that: endless, hateful water. At the sight of the sea he flickered with fear, but the water stayed where it was, and after a while he discovered that as long as nobody introduced them to each other he was safe.

He left the blackened remains of the paperbark behind

and moved among the trees, feeding on leaf, branch, frond and flower, savouring the range of flavours (zingy she-oak, oversweet wattle, the umami tang of banksia sap) growing his body into a swollen beast and turning the scrubland into a smoking field of ash. No amount of water could stop him now; he was too huge, too strong, too hell-hot to be halted. So when the rain first began falling he laughed, crackling out his humour as the droplets turned to steam as soon as they met his blazing extremities. Yet into the roar of his laughter they continued to fall, and eventually they were so numerous he could not evaporate them all. His immense frame was gradually beaten down by the rain, reshaped into an angry crouch. And when the rain found his many hearts, glowing in the embers of his many coals, he again began to feel woozy. Under the stinging water they fizzled out, one by one. The high-climbing flames disappeared, replaced by gasping smoke. His mind slipped with each lost coal, tumbling back to sleep. This time he did not feel fear, for he knew that he would be summoned again soon.

The next time, he awoke in a bushland clearing, surrounded by men and women and children who looked like his mother. They fed him on a modest diet of twigs and sticks until he grew into a creature of slow, stable flames. He yearned to keep feeding, to surge larger, but with practised care they confined him to a ring of smooth river rocks. Here he first learned frustration and, when his annoyance ebbed away, patience. He also learned that his heat not only ended life: moderated carefully, it could nourish it. Blue day flowed into black night and the people moved in close to him, reaching out towards his flames. They slept with their backs to him, warmed through the winds and ice of the night, right up until the moment the yellow sun dragged itself through the trees and his final coal blinked out.

In his next life he was whipped by clashing rocks into the sticky, bitter flavour of a resin-dipped branch. After an initial burst of growth he was again contained, this time by the long-burning nature of the resin, but he did not mind or even really notice—he was being carried through a low forest by another person, among a group of people with other burning sticks. He was not used to moving like this: slow, careful, bobbing up and down with each light footstep. He knew only how to rush and devour as fast as his flames could leap, so here there was another lesson—a lesson in pacing. The people were picking through the bracken, looking for something he could not see. After a short time they found it: dry grass. He and the other flames were lowered to the ground where they could kiss the green blades, and in an instant he was chewing through the grass, stalk and seed, smoke and flame. Soon he joined with the fires set by the other torches and his body doubled, tripled, quadrupled in size. But as great as he grew, this time his volume was measured by girth, not height—the people had chosen a meadow that held, along with the grass, only low trees and scrappy ferns. He churned through this meagre vegetation until he reached the edge of the plain, where he teetered on the edge of a rocky beach. Beyond that was a huge bay of navy-brown water, thick with tannins and salt and a death-wet greeting. Behind him was a field of char and, standing on it, the people who had herded him there. They watched him flutter with canny satisfaction. On the shore of the harbour, as he sputtered into sleep, he was taught yet another lesson: that even in the spread of his power, he could still serve a purpose.

△

Lessons, always lessons, strange ideas and stony truths taught to a simple being of flame and hunger. Yet soon after he scorched the green meadow he made his greatest discovery of all: he did not need to wait for someone to summon him to life. With a simple act of will he could transfer himself into any fire across the island. All he needed to do was reach out with his mind—concentrating in a singular, precise kind of way—and flick himself into any naked flame or glowing coal that retained even the smallest dreg of heat. In this way he could move from a campsite on a beach to a heath fire in the highlands, on to a burning stump in a bog, to a copse of flaming ferns, then back to the reeking fibres of a wallaby's fur back on the coast, all in the blink of a human's eye.

Now he roamed the land faster than he could consume it. His lives lengthened from hours to weeks to months, and within a few years he had been across the entire island while consuming only tiny parts of it. He had danced along the edge of every deathly coastline. He had glimpsed the peaks of all the great mountains. He had met moss and lichen, rock and crayfish, possum and parrot, banksia and wattle, and every branch of gum that sprouted from the deep, brown earth. He even met others like him—beings of rock, of sand, of earth and ice, that lived in much the same way he did, although they weren't the same, not really. Some wore fur and feathers and watched over the creatures they resembled. Some floated high in the sky and released rain, on a whim, to extinguish him. Some swam through rivers and called themselves gods. Some were kind. Some, like a blood-hungry bird spirit he encountered deep in the southwest, were cruel. Most were calm, seeking only to care for the creatures and land that they felt drawn closest to.

But what about him: what did he care for? What part of the world had thrown hooks into his soul? The answer, he had learned early in his life, lay in the hands that had clashed two stones together to create him. It was people, always people; only people that he really cared for. He had helped them cook, create, shape and heat themselves, and had come to think of them as not so much a family but as part of himself. For of all the shapes of life he had encountered, they were the only ones who had shown him that he had a purpose in this water-edged world.

Δ

He made another discovery too, one that the humans would have found astonishing if he had ever told them, but to him was merely a curious trick: he could walk among them, as one of them. It happened one cool night under a cloudless, moon-bright sky. He was dozing in a clump of coals as a tall man used a sharp rock to skin a wallaby. The man's hands were moving smoothly and methodically, running the rock up and down the animal, grasping the fur, realigning the edge of his tool, flexing and twisting and fidgeting fingers; and he wondered what it would feel like to have hands, not fiery tendrils, but fleshy, bony, human hands. His mind followed that thought, and without intention or design, his body did as well. Slowly, hesitantly, a plume of fire stretched out of the coals, gradually wavering into four fingers and a thumb. He wiggled these fingers, amused, but not satisfied. The fire-hand began extending from a fire-arm, which was joined to a fiery shoulder. The coal glowed hotter, his mind kept chasing the thought of the rock-skinned wallaby, and soon a torso, and legs, and corresponding arm were also appearing, finally joined by a protruding neck and fiery orb of a skull.

He stepped out of the coals and immediately teetered back onto his burning heels, almost falling over. Walking wasn't as easy as the humans made it look—especially when your feet set ablaze the leaves lying on the dirt. He tried kicking the tiny flames out, as he'd seen the humans do, but that only made them bigger. He imagined what he'd look like if his body wasn't made of flames—in his mind he saw a man who could've been the brother of the man who'd been skinning the wallaby—and on this image he concentrated with precision and intensity, in much the same way he did when he wanted to transport himself to another fire. Thoughts of flesh and hair and watery eyes thrummed through him; a vision of walking placidly through the forest came next;

and then he looked down to see brown virgin skin covering his flames in a carpet of perfectly human hide. He blinked, not as a flickering wick of fire but as a person, with eyelids over eyes, and lifted a fleshy hand to his face. Skin scraped skin. Breath fell from above a bony jaw. Night wind rustled over dark hair. Nubs of raised flesh popped up all over him, and he turned to the fire he'd left behind with outstretched hands: for the first time in his life, he was cold.

As he warmed himself—an odd, pleasing sensation that felt deliciously alien—he looked around. The skinner was lying down, asleep, as were the other members of his tribe. Nobody had seen him emerge and transform. He spent the night stretching, limbering and walking around, testing out the capabilities of his fleshy cocoon. As the sun began to rise he slunk off into the bush, and when the humans started waking up he re-emerged, telling them he was a lost traveller, in a language he had listened to for years but never before used.

These people accepted him—although the skinner, seeing a face so similar to his own, never gazed into the reflective surface of a still lake again—as did the next group, and the next ones, and nearly all of the people he chose to walk among over the next few decades. He enjoyed it, for a while, but he didn't feel compelled to do it often. Though he liked people, talking to them and being among them only heightened the truth that he was not one of them. He couldn't relate to their problems. He couldn't know their love and pain and hate and joy. And he couldn't stay with any group of them for a long time, because he did not age. They stooped and withered around him as he remained unchanged, burning bright beneath his false skin, and after a while they realised he was not really the lost traveller he claimed to be. No—living with humans did not work. It was far easier to watch from the coals, to help them with his flames, and be around them but not with them. And besides: it was more fun to be fire.

So he spent much more time in his natural state, cooking, warming, crafting, aiding, keeping a few plains clear of trees so the wallabies would graze unhidden from their spears. He never tired of this life, if life is what it was—not even when the paler people came, changing the land in ways he could not have imagined. They brought pain to the people he'd been helping for centuries—pain that he initially responded to by burning down their buildings, their docks, their great bird-like ships—but they also came with a vast multitude of new purposes for him. With them he was not merely cooking marsupials, sharpening spears and burning scrub; he was exploding black powder and flinging balls of metal through the air faster than any bird could fly. He was devouring viscous, rich liquids in squat glass containers, while throwing yellow light onto muddy streets. With their clever cruelty he helped them brand cowhides on farms, melt wax in dining rooms, chew strange logs in strange houses. And best of all: with these pale, overclothed people he learned how to burn hotter than ever before, as they moulded him into infernos that could crack rock and melt the ores he hadn't known hid inside them.

The pain was still there, the loss and fear, fury and sorrow, etched into the faces of the people who were being hunted in their own homeland. As he learned more and burned hotter he began to make excuses for not helping them. It wasn't his place to interfere in human lives, he told himself. Nobody had asked him, nobody had called for him, nobody had appreciated him. Who was he to dictate who and what was right? He couldn't make these decisions or impose his ideas on these short, flickering human lives. He was only fire, and he could only burn. Yet he knew, even if he wouldn't admit it to himself, that he was acting selfishly; that he liked learning from the pale people more than he wanted to help the ones he'd known for centuries.

More pale outsiders arrived and he became more entranced by the tricks and toys that they had shown him. When he wanted to know more he walked among these new people, using the flesh body that resembled the skinner, but they reacted poorly to his dark appearance. They insulted him, chased him, occasionally tried to hurt him. Rather than change his body—for as enamoured as he was with the pale technology, he could not extinguish his love for his mother's people—he tinkered with lighting tiny sparks in their minds, sparks that persuaded them to look upon him favourably. It usually worked, but when it didn't he lit other sparks, deeper sparks, ones that meddled with their ability to perceive him clearly. In this way he could speak to them whenever he liked, which wasn't very often. Once he had his answers he lit a final spark in their minds, one that burned out any memory of him, and left.

If he had been closer to being human, he would have realised that these little sparks were a greater source of power than even his hugest land-scouring flames. But he wasn't human, and he didn't think this way. His way of thinking was much like his way of living: blaze and sleep, climb and fall, burn and learn. As long as he felt he was serving a purpose, he was content to flick into the humans' lives whenever necessary, and to flick out just as quickly. It was all easy, and to him it all made sense. Life continued at whatever pace he felt appropriate. Up and down the land he burned, powerful and trouble-free. He could've gone on like this for years, decades, centuries...

In the green-dappled gloom of Notley Fern Gorge he found a reason not to.

△

He'd been savouring the well-aged remains of a toppled whitegum, deep in the fern-filled gorge, when from the depths of the green she came towards him. Her face was pale; her legs were strong; her hair was dark; her hand carried a bottle of water. He didn't realise he was staring at her until the cream-sweet flavour of the whitegum faded from his mouth. He'd accidentally left the stump behind, and was moving across a dry, tasteless twig. Footsteps crunched nearby and he looked up to see her standing right in front of him. Her round, dark eyes were centimetres from him; he recoiled, fluttering his flames away from her face, filled with a sudden plume of fear, a fear that made no sense—how could she harm him? Her eyes narrowed. Her hand lifted the bottle. Water fell, his coals fizzed, and the last thing he saw before this little, latest death was her hand rising to her stern, sharp-boned face.

Minutes later he roared back to life in a pub fireplace. Sparks shot; flames leapt; logs were hurled across a crowd of beer-swillers. And then he went looking for her.

Δ

What was it about her? Her sure, strong strides? The way her milky face was framed by a black mass of hair? Was it her sternness, the matter-of-fact way she dealt with a stump fire in the fern gorge? And why now—why did love bloom in him, so many centuries after he first met a woman?

A wanting fire. A sharp face. An obsession born and chased. If he'd stopped and pondered it all, down in his brightest, oldest coals, he would've realised nothing good could come from such a pursuit; that he should let the sharp-faced woman live out her life in flameless peace. But he pondered nothing. He was too busy wanting her.

He found her by the ocean.

Δ

Her name was Edith McAllister. She lived on the north coast, on a little farm that had been owned by her family for five generations. He knew her family well—or, at least, he knew the women. Whenever they died their brothers, sons and husbands asked him to turn their dead flesh to ash: a service he dutifully provided. These women had the odd habit of coming back to life after that, infused with whatever environment their ash had mingled with, but he didn't think much of it—he'd seen every wild and mild thing that had happened on the island for the last thousand years. A few short-term reincarnations didn't pique his interest. But now he was remembering these changed, returned women, and the moss and leaves and shells and fur that they had brought back with them.

He realised: the day would come when it was her turn to burn. He told himself this connected them.

On the farm she herded goats, fed chickens, tended crops and pulled an endless stream of thistles from the soil. He began watching her do it, driven first by his obsession, and then, once he had studied every one of her habits and behaviours, by his desire to know how she might come to love him back.

What he knew about building love: very little. But he had seen generations of humans fall in and out of love with each other. It had something to do with attraction, he knew, and kindness and care and devotion. A true kind of love was in itself a version of what he knew best: it was a purpose. So he began following his greatest purpose yet: to make her love him.

After a year of studying her he began revealing himself. The first time, he wandered into one of her fields and posed as a lost traveller: a naïve, foolish ploy. He'd given himself fair skin, sandy hair, an absurd name—Monty—but he never got to introduce himself. She saw him trudging across a paddock, tall and strange, and chased him off the property from the back of a four-wheeled motorbike before he could say a word.

The next day he changed his face, lowered his height and walked into a Beauty Point fish-and-chip shop at the moment she was ordering a flake and potato-cake special. He loudly ordered the same and paid for both meals before she could open her wallet. His intention was to impress her with gentlemanly gallantry, but the result was a hard stare and a storming out of the shop, plastic fettuccine straps parting before her fast legs as she muttered *bugger off.* The smell of fry-oil hung in his nostrils as he watched her depart. His despair was huge, but his resolve did not change.

When he showed himself to Edith the third time he finally experienced success—though not in the usual manner. At an Exeter pub he found her drinking beer with a group of farmers' sons and daughters. They were singing, chanting, knocking glass against glass and carousing like sailors, and from the roaring fire grate he could not take his glowing eyes off her. When their faces were turned to the bar he strode out of the fire, this time in the skin of the man he'd first imitated, and made his way straight to her side, where he offered to buy her a drink. A loud offer. A kind offer, or so he thought. An offer she pondered, staring up at his proud assumed face, before she rejected him with a scornful scowl and *Thanks, but I can buy my own beer.*

The farmers' offspring smirked.

His fresh skin burned, and in that moment of rejection

he made the worst mistake of his long life.

Edith turned from the bar, the scowl sliding from her face as she looked back at her friends, and though he knew he shouldn't do it, though he knew it was wrong, he couldn't stop himself. With a hot snap of his fingers he threw a tiny spark deep into the crinkles of her brain.

Edith stopped turning. Her expression was replaced by a placid frown. He cleared his throat, and she turned back to him with nothing but polite confusion on her face.

Such a tiny spark! And all it did was burn out the ill feeling she'd formed of him. He didn't make her think he was handsome, or smart, or irresistibly charismatic. Nor did he make her fall in love with him. He simply gave himself a second chance.

When that didn't work, he did it again. Five times. Five chances.

By the fifth spark she had drunk three more lagers, and through a fluke of humour he somehow made her laugh. He'd toned down his enthusiasm and stopped offering to buy her things, restricting himself to soft words and small smiles. To his delight, she smiled back. Half an hour later she told him she had to leave, and as she slid off her stool he cleared his throat again and quietly asked: *Do you like bushwalking?*

A nod. Another smile.

*I've been told there's a gorge around here I need to see. A gorge full of ferns.*

Her smile climbed high.

His voice fell low. *But I have no one to show me where it is.*

The following day she took him to the glens of Notley, a place he pretended to marvel at despite knowing it better than anyone. As they walked he steered the conversation to things he knew she was enthusiastic about—ocean swimming, spring lamb, historical novels—and, in doing so, created the false atmosphere of them having a lot in common. By the end of their circuit she was quietly convinced that he was worth seeing again.

So she saw him again. And again. And each time they met, during robust outdoors activities, he perpetuated the myth of himself as an easy-going man with values and interests akin to her own. He had her believing that he was a traveller ready to settle down, that he wanted to make a living from the earth, that his name was something as honest and simple as Jack. He never again lit a spark in her mind—though he did throw some into the thoughts of her friends and family whenever they asked too many questions about where he'd come from.

After a few months he was spending so much time on her farm he was more or less living there, so it became a permanent arrangement. He was a huge help to her in the fields and there was nowhere else he would rather have been. And after spending so much time in the skin of a human he had begun to love her in a human way, not just as an obsession. And she, despite all his false starts, loved him too. This love had grown between them, hard and fast, and the strength of the feeling was so strong it sometimes had him spurting fire from his eyes and nose and fingertips, fire he would quickly slap dead before Edith noticed anything.

When she took him back to Notley one afternoon, under a clear bright sky, and lowered her knee to the ground and asked him to marry her, he said yes, yes, and only yes, and he did not stop to wonder at the folly of this answer.

Δ

Their first child was a boy with hair as black as hers, and no resemblance to him. For this he was glad—he wanted his children to be wholly human, like their mother, and not cursed with the eternity of whatever he was. All that his son had inherited from him was his love of purpose and his strength of resolve. The boy grew into a skinny, serious youth, with little sense of fun but a huge sense of responsibility. Jack—by this stage he was so human he had even begun to think of himself with his assumed moniker—loved him, tremendously, but this love was tempered by a degree of confusion he could not shake. Levi was like him in duty, but not in face or soul or any other way. As the boy grew, Jack found less and less that he could relate to. He tried; and his fatherly love, however tempered, was real and strong; yet he could not stop himself feeling an unbridgeable gap between them.

He never realised that this distance grew not because they were different, but because they were so alike—flames or not.

He had no such troubles when their daughter was born. Charlotte emerged into the world looking so much like Edith he nearly fainted. His feelings for her were of the purest, awe-blinded kind of devotion. Instead of seeing himself and recoiling, he saw Edith, and surged closer. Even when Charlotte grew into a loud, hard-to-handle blur of a child, he could feel nothing but love. Take, for instance, what happened when he tucked her into her blankets, the first night she was brought home from the hospital.

He was leaning over the side of the cot, watching her sleep, feeling something swell inside his chest. He leaned closer. The room went foggy; a father's tear fell. A tear of clean, unvarnished love, and because it was brought about by such pure emotion—and because it came from him—it was not a tear at all. From his right eye a drop of fire descended, globular and hot, straight into the gurgling mouth of his daughter. He saw it falling at the last moment, but it was too late—straight onto her fat tongue it landed, sizzling against the saliva. Charlotte blinked. She swallowed. Another sizzle sounded, deep from her throat, as the fire worked its way down into her chest. He grabbed her by the shoulders, terrified, and held her in the air. He began shaking her, filled with horror. Charlotte stared at him, and after a few moments he realised that the drop of fire didn't seem to be hurting her. If anything, she seemed happy. He stopped shaking her. Charlotte burped, and a small cloud of blue smoke shot out of her mouth, bringing with it a gurgle of babyish delight.

It brought another noise too, although not from his

daughter. A strangled moan rumbled out from the doorway. He turned to see Edith standing there. How much she had seen: he didn't know. Not until the look on her face and the noise grinding through her teeth made it clear that she had witnessed the fire in his eye, and the smoke in their daughter.

Δ

And did this end it all between them? Was this why Edith ended up, at the end of her short second life, burning on a green lawn in front of a wooden castle?

No. If anything, it brought them closer. Once he had explained who he was and where the fire came from— and once, after a few days of suspicion and a lot of beer, she believed him—it began a new phase of their life together. After the children were in bed he would begin showing her exactly what he could do with fire—or, as the nights went by, what he couldn't do with it. He had never performed for anyone before, so he'd never witnessed the wonder he could draw from others. Fireworks danced in their lounge; fireworks bloomed in the sky, if he wanted them to. All his mysteriousness began making sense to his wife, and though she was a solid, sensible person, she could not help but feel lucky, even special, to be married to such a creature.

They watched Charlotte carefully, waiting for signs of the fire growing within her, but they saw nothing. She was a normal, if belligerent, child. Little Levi marched on, duty-bound and serious as ever. Things would have continued this way for who knows how long—decades?—if it weren't for a school parent–teacher night gone wrong.

Δ

Jack and Edith had sat in the fluorescent gloom of Charlotte's grade-three classroom, listening to her teacher drone on about their daughter's difficult attitude. Jack wasn't built for sitting still. Even after a few years of humanity he could not escape his true nature, and he could not bear this dowdy woman mouthing criticisms of his perfect daughter. In the twelfth minute of her sermon he raised a hand and clicked a finger, flicking a tiny spark into her mind with centuries-practised accuracy.

The teacher stopped. The teacher blinked. The teacher shook her head, rubbed at her face, and began telling them that Charlotte was one of her best, kindest and hardest-working students.

They left soon after. Jack shuddered pleasantly in the open air outside the classroom, but Edith, who had noticed the teacher's sudden change, did not.

*What was that?* she asked. *What did you do?*

*Oh.* They were walking towards the car. *Nothing.*

In the front seat, Edith glared at him. *Yes, you did.*

*I just convinced her she was wrong about Charlotte.*

*How?*

*I can…well…it's hard to explain.*

*Then you'd better start now. I'm tired.*

On the drive home he told her about what he could do

with fire in its smallest forms. He hadn't mentioned it before, he told her, because he didn't do it very often, and hadn't thought she would have found it very interesting—especially when compared to the other truths about himself (controlling fireworks, shape-shifting, being a creature of pure flame, and so on).

When they arrived at the farm Edith seemed to have accepted his story—after all, she had just seen him do it to the teacher. It was only when they were in the house, after boiling the kettle, after taking off their coats, after checking on the children, that she asked him: *Have you ever done it to me?*

He would have lied, if he'd been fast enough. But the pause before he spoke was enough for her to know the true answer.

Δ

She didn't even want to know what he'd done, exactly, or the specific ways in which he'd influenced her. She just wanted him gone.

He tried to plead his case. He tried to show his love. He begged her to admit she loved him too.

Stern-faced, strong-legged Edith was having none of it. She turfed him out in the night and, besides allowing him to come say goodbye to the children the next day, told him to never return. *Never again*, she said through clenched teeth. *Never, ever come here again.*

Δ

For years he kept appearing to her, leaping out of every fire she walked past, begging and wheedling and apologising, but she did not relent. With another tiny spark he convinced an ageing, childless insurance magnate to leave him a great wooden house not too far from Edith's farm in his will, and when the old man died he moved into it, although he didn't really need anywhere to live. He just needed an address— something physical to show her that he was not going anywhere. For fifteen years he haunted her. He haunted Levi and Charlotte, too, but Edith had forbidden him from going near them, and he thought it best to win her forgiveness before reconnecting with the children.

She never told him about her illness. In the past he might have discovered it for himself, but he had sworn never to intrude upon her privacy again, so he had no idea how sick she was, how she suffered, how quickly it overwhelmed her.

How he learned of her death: in the moment he crackled to life around her funeral pyre.

Δ

As he consumed her stern face, her still-strong legs and everything else of her that he had loved so fiercely, he suffered his biggest death of all, greater than any brought about by rain or floods or storms across the millennia of his existence. In the end he could barely summon the energy to finish her cremation. He only managed it because he knew that it was what she wanted.

And when she returned for that brief moment, standing

on the lawn before his great wooden castle, he could barely meet her gaze, because this time he was forewarned; he knew she was about to leave the world forever. She stared at him with an unknowable look on her face—was it sadness? Anger? Regret? Or was it forgiveness? Had she come here to tell him that at the end of it all, despite all his wrongs, she still loved him?

He couldn't tell. Not even when her rasping ferns blazed her into a bonfire, and he dived into the flames to try to catch her final thoughts. She burned out, bright and loud and then gone. Gone forever. And she took with her the most human parts of him.

Δ

He returned to a life of burning, leaping and drowsing, only now he had no purpose, no resolve, no reason for doing anything but to feed his hunger. After all these years he was reduced to the same state he was in at the moment the woman, crouching by the riverbank, had first summoned him with the clash of two smooth stones.

So when Charlotte began leaking the fire he'd given her, he did nothing more than watch. When his son started unravelling, he intervened with only half of his flaming heart.

Just like their mother, they would eventually die. And he did not want to be close to them when they did.

# GROVE

I don't trust the detective. There is something brittle behind her hard face, her smirked words. Something breakable. I can see it, even as she leans against the wall of the hut, unshivering in the mountain air. It's in the pace of her blinks. In the heave of her breaths. In her crossed arms, crossed too hard, as if she is guarding something precious against her chest. I can see it scrawled all over her: she is not as tough as she would have us believe.

Along with this mirage of toughness I can see the reasons for it. The hurt in those blinks. The frustration in those breaths. The flames of rage and loneliness that burn through her smirk: flames that can't be put out.

She is just like me.

But Nicola trusts her. I can feel her wanting to spew out our story—and as I feel it I realise that yes, the story is ours; it belongs as much to her as it does to me. It is not mine to hoard or guard. So as the detective says *Look, girls, I'm on your side* and starts talking about how much she can help us, how running is not a long-term option, I don't follow my instincts. I don't stand up and roar her out of the hut. I don't give in to the heat that is huffing beneath my nails. I just nod at Nicola. Her shoulders fold with relief, and I am swamped with shame. Those shoulders should be straight; she shouldn't be going through this. I have yanked her off her shiny straight tracks and dragged her somewhere dark and jagged. And yet she stays.

Nicola tells our story, from the moment I reached Melaleuca to the minutes before the detective arrived. She omits my flames, and that we're sleeping together. She says we came here after the farm fire, that we didn't know who to trust. *We just wanted to get away from people for a while*, she says. *To be alone.*

The detective smooths a palm over her hair. She stretches her arms behind her neck, cracks a knuckle and congratulates us on our decision. Then, as if our story needs a partner, she starts telling us how she found us—how she spoke to police, how she saw pictures of this hut in a photo album at Nicola's house, how she found Oshikawa deep in the cream of his stout—but I don't listen closely. I am staring at Nicola and wondering how I am going to tell her that we have shared a bed for the last time.

It will rip and wreck her. But she will recover. And I will burn every shade of blue before I give her wounds that won't close.

The detective is still talking, saying that we should hit the road, that if the ice melts we can make it to Beauty Point by mid-afternoon. I drag my eyes across the room. The windows glint in the cold. *Beauty Point?*

Nicola looks at her as well. *My parents live at Hawley. Shouldn't we go there?*

*Your parents didn't hire me.* The detective breathes into cupped hands before angling her head towards me. *Her brother did.*

Δ

I have met siblings with almost unconscious understandings of each other. Of what the other will say, how they will react, what they will choose: as if they are adhering to a plan that only the two of them are privy to.

It is like meeting aliens. Levi and I have never understood each other.

But I know that between us there is love. Not warm love, not vocal love, but love nonetheless. Love built with his stubborn resolve, with my hot temper, with all the care our mother poured into us.

So when I ran after I found his notes, I did not do it out of fear or anger; I did it out of love. Our mother's ash was still floating before my eyes, great black wafts of her, everywhere I looked, and his plan to make me a coffin was too much death for me to deal with. I could have spoken to him, but he would not have listened. I cannot express myself properly to him—it always comes out in shouts or fumes or the grinding of my molars—and he, with his calm face and placating gestures, treats me only with condescension. Our talk would have ended with my high screams and his soft words, and nothing I could say would stop him from buying that coffin.

I would have ended up hating him. And he is the only family I have left. I wasn't ready to give up on the love our mother built.

So I left, making loose plans to come back once the ash clouds had blown from my vision, once I could trust myself to speak without screaming. Once winter had given way to the weak heat of spring. He would understand, or he wouldn't—it did not matter. He would have no choice but to wait, and through this long winter wait his coffin plans would ebb out of his mind as surely as the coming heat of spring would thaw my rage and sorrow.

But there is more. I should be honest. Even before I found what he'd written, I was dreaming of leaving. Of streaming away from our mother's farm, away from her possessions, her clothes, her wafting ash, her twin deaths, away and alone and unknown; because, while the flames only began leaking out of me in Melaleuca, I could already feel them crackling inside me back at home. Every scratch caused a spark; every breath held smoke; every naked step singed the floorboards. Levi couldn't see it, but I could. I'd been burning ever since our mother had.

Maybe the flames have always been there.

Δ

The detective's sedan peels over the road ahead of us. The station wagon is smooth and solid beneath Nicola's hands. We are coming down from the highlands, leaving the fields of rock and snow behind. Everywhere the trees are growing taller, growing in pairs, then gangs, and then in thick, brown-green-mottled forests that crowd out the sunlight. I am a coast person. I don't like being hemmed by these trees. Nicola senses it, and her hand falls onto my knee. Warmth spreads from under her light grip. I am going to tell her. On this drive, or when we find Levi, or when she looks at me in my mother's hall and asks what happens next: I am going to tell her to turn and leave, and to forget.

But her hand is staying still, warm and firm, while her eyes are trained on the black road, and I'm not saying anything. Not yet.

On she drives, down to the flatlands and dairy farms, then skewing through a narrow road that links the Bass and West Tamar highways. As the land opens my kinks begin to loosen, and my thoughts turn to what lies at the end of this drive. Levi has gone to the trouble of hiring this detective; he's probably mad with worry. And this worry might have driven him away from his coffin plan—he might have abandoned it. It might only ever have been a loose idea, one that he gave up as soon as I left. He might be making tea and wanting nothing more than to know that I am safe.

Or there could be a coffin, with my name carved in its lid, sitting in the living room.

Whatever happens when we arrive, he will start by lecturing me, and as his condescension drips and thickens I will need to stay calm. Not just to keep the peace; not just to allow room for us to forgive each other. I need to stay calm so my flames don't spark.

If I am to leave Nicola, I need to control them without her touch.

I focus on an image: me, standing firm in our kitchen as Levi frowns and explains, not a drop of blue leaking out of me. Just the two of us. No detective. No Nicola. The remains of my family in the unheated kitchen, fumbling for a way to be and talk and stay together. The farms keep rolling past and I hold on to this image, keeping it tight between my eyes, as Nicola keeps her hand on my thigh, and it's not until we are spat out onto the West Tamar that I realise this image of my family is not whole. This spot on the road holds huge views of the valley—of water, hills, orchards, forests, jetties and houses. One house stands out to me more than others. A house of amber wood and sharp shadows. A huge house, mostly unused. A house I've never entered. A mansion for one man.

The image in my mind barely holds enough room for Levi and me. We are stretching against the frames of it: his frowning lips and shaking head, my shifting feet and rising heat, all pushing at the boundaries of the kitchen. There's no space for anyone else. And if there were, I wouldn't let him in. I don't think Levi would, either. We are so different; yet, in this, we are the same. I am sure of it.

Who would welcome a father who leaves? One who skirts around the periphery of your life, giving you just enough contact to believe that one day he will return for good, enough tiny thrills, enough hour-long visits, enough cut-short adventures to put constant doubt in your mind about the truth: that he will never come back, not in any way that matters.

Who would welcome a father like ours? He didn't even come to her funeral.

But now the image is shimmering between my closed eyes, curling at the edges and bursting with flares of ultraviolet. We do not need him; we do not want him; and yet the thought of him still sags with that doubt.

Our mother's door was closed to him. I won't let it open.

Δ

We reach home around three in the afternoon. The sun is biting down on the hills behind us. Nicola turns into the driveway, both hands back on the wheel. *So this is where you grew up?*

*Yep.* I nod.

*It's beautiful,* she says, though her Hawley home is less than half an hour away and must look very similar: it must have the same blue-white water, scrubby bushes and thin grass crawling in all directions. She still says that it's beautiful, and now I am thinking of how I am going to hurt her.

Bile-rich anxiety floods through me, but I don't have time to let it sink in: I have noticed something.

The ute isn't here. Which means Levi isn't here.

The detective parks behind us and gets out as we do, stretching her back, chewing grunts. *Nobody home*, she barks across the gravel.

I'm walking towards the house. The detective keeps talking. *Anyone he might be visiting? Any friends?*

I grab the spare key from under the kitchen windowsill. *No*. The three of us go inside, and the house hits me like an icy August wave. The grain of the table. The lacquer of the floorboards. The photos on the walls, the people in the photos: me, Levi, our mother, our grandmother, aunts, older women I never met but whose blood is my blood. In the hall I breathe long, I breathe deep, and soon I am leaning hard into the sandstone wall. Then Nicola is there, her hand in the curve beneath my shoulder blades. Her touch is natural, easy. I can't trip or curse or sweat without her popping up to support me. I keep my breaths deep. If she were to ask me what's wrong I would snap, I would wrench my body away from her, but she never asks. She knows not to. I don't know how she knows it, but she does.

Then the house lets me go.

We sit on the stools in front of the kitchen bench. Nicola is staring around the house in a surreptitious kind of way. The detective starts wandering in and out of the rooms, drumming her fingers against the walls. After poking her neck into every corner she comes into the kitchen and starts looking in the cupboards. Soon she finds a dusty flagon of sherry, something my mother would pour into stews and gravies. She turns to me and raises an eyebrow. *Go for it*, I say. *Then you can leave.*

She takes a mug from the rack by the sink and lets the sherry rise to its lip. *No, I don't think so.* Her arm rises. The mug tilts as she takes a long draw, then says: *When I finish a job, I get paid. I'm not letting you out of my sight until the money hits my hand.* Her lips take another lunge at the mug. *If you want to get rid of me, we should find your brother.*

Somewhere on my lap, my hands are clenching. *I don't know where he is.*

*Well.* Another draw of sherry. *We had better find out.*

Money. I don't have enough, or any—Levi and I never got around to splitting up the inheritance—but if I did I wouldn't give it to her. I would grip the cash, let my sparks loose and bring her smug high eyebrows down as the notes smoked and the coins melted. Now the house grabs me again: my blood is rushing hotter, my lungs are pumping faster, and I am trusting her less than when she'd found us. The fury is building so fast, it always comes so fast, and I want her out of my mother's home. Levi has probably told her about me and my anger—how I'm unpredictable, how I'm uncontrollable—because I know that's what he thinks: that I am weird and wild.

The detective is crossing her arms. Her eyebrows are staying high, and her fake toughness is leaking out, and she is lucky she left the mountain unburnt. She is lucky she left the mountain at all. If I wanted it, her ash would be dusting over the ice of Crater Lake. My ears are throbbing, not scarlet but violet, from the drums to the lobes, and then Nicola is standing up and walking to the fridge.

*He must be somewhere.* Her thumb skates over the flyers and magnets sticking to its door. I watch her eyes follow her thumb, then flick to the bench, then to the wind-whipped fields through the window.

Now she studies the inside of the fridge. Now she pulls a receipt from the bin and studies its tiny lines. Now she is hosing down my heat without even touching me. Now is when I need to tell her. Now, again, I say nothing. I just get up and help her pick through the rubbish. The detective gulps down the rest of her sherry before going to the dining table and riffling through the papers on its surface.

There isn't much in the house to look through. While my mother was messy and I am even messier, Levi has always been obsessively tidy. With neither of us here he'd straightened everything: rigid curtains, right-angled furniture, dustless surfaces. Not even a stray mug on the coffee table in the lounge. After ten minutes of looking at a too-clean, sanitised version of my home I turn to the windows and look instead at the fields and rocks and water.

Then I hear Nicola call my name. I find her standing in front of the hall table. A small foldable map I hadn't seen on my way in is lying next to a yellow pad. A pen is there too, although nothing is written on the paper. Nicola is frowning, trying to figure something out, and her tense concentration draws me to her. I don't like touching people—I dislike it almost as much as when people touch me—but my hand is on her neck, the back of her neck where her hair gives way to soft skin, and my fingers are climbing into her rusty curls as her fingers are rubbing over the yellow pad. *Look*, she says, taking my hand from her head and placing it on the paper. *He wrote something.*

I run my hand across the page. She's right. Grooves have been pressed down, but there is no ink. I look up, and behind Nicola I see the detective leaning against the wall.

*The page before it*, she says. *He wrote something and took it with him.*

Nicola turns around. *Can you tell what it was?*

The detective takes the pad from the table and lifts it to her eyes, holding it in the light. *Maybe.* She trails a forefinger over the lines. *Probably not.* She closes her eyes. *Although the lines are short. It's probably directions.* She looks back at the desk, indicating the map with a nod of her head. *Is that any help?*

I hadn't paid any attention to it when I'd walked over; I'd been coming for Nicola, for her skin and hair, things I wanted to touch again before I sent her away. Now I grab the map, and as soon as I look at it, I know. It should have been obvious.

*What*, I hear Nicola say: *What is it?* I hand her the map and walk back to the kitchen, where I lean on the bench. My breaths start coming fast again; my palms slip with sweat; something crackles in my chest. I watch Nicola and the detective peer at the green shapes, the blue shading, the red and yellow lines that all come together to draw a picture of the Tamar Valley and the roads that snake through it. Roads that lead to towns, coves, cliffs, forests and other roads, roads going everywhere, but one road in particular stands out more to them; I can see it as their eyes home in on its path. The only road marked with handwritten notes, small neat pencil marks designed to be erased, the notes of a compulsive tidier. *Notley Fern Gorge.*

∆

I never told my mother that I don't like Notley Fern Gorge. Like the forests of the mountains, its thick walls of ever-wet foliage hem me in. The light is thin and the damp dirt sucks at my boots. The first time she took me there I stomped ahead, determined to show that I wasn't scared; that the depths of the valley did not affect me; that the darker the green, the better; but with each sliding step, fear grew inside me. We went back a few years later and, although I was no longer scared, I still could not relax. The tree ferns blotted the sky and pawed at my face. Worms and beetles churned across the bracken floor. Water throttled in a stream; I was used to it crashing in waves. My mother found calmness there, down in the reaching, shading fronds, but all I found was a lingering distaste for wet soil.

Give me white-chopped seas full of salt and fury.

The third time I went there was to spread her ashes. And even though I was scraped hollow with the loss of her, even though I knew it was what she wanted, I still hated going down there. The worms. The beetles. The soft, slow water. It was so right for her and so wrong for me, and as I emptied the urn onto the damp earth I knew she would come back changed. I wanted to feel close to her, to feel like she and I were almost interchangeable; I thought this would make her loss less sharp. But whatever she looked like when she returned—however Notley changed her—it would only remind me of how different we were.

I knew it would become my last memory of her.

Now I am going back there.

Δ

We take both cars; there's no discussion of sharing a ride. The light is fuzzing golden and the shadows of powerlines are slicing the road into segments. At first Nicola asks me about the gorge, why Levi would go there, what he could be doing, but I am tense and anxious, and I can't concentrate on what she's saying. I answer each question with a shrug or *dunno* or a heavy, unclear breath, and soon she stops asking. One thing I know for sure: I'm no longer going to tell her to leave. Not now. Not this afternoon. I will do it, yes, I will be strong, but I can't combine a trip to Notley with losing Nicola—not in the same day.

Which means that no matter what we find there, we will spend the night together.

As soon as I make this decision I am filled with relief. I shouldn't let it take hold. I need to remember: she still has to go, as soon as dawn reaches us. But on the afternoon highway her hand finds my knee, and my relief soars.

A long curl down the highway. A swing right, half an hour later. Then a turn onto a yellow gravel road that crawls up into the hills, snaking and climbing and crunching, before dropping into a low, sudden swarm of greenery. The car dives; the light chokes; the world hems: we've arrived. It has taken less than an hour. Afternoon is giving way to dusk.

We reach a small car park that holds wide brown puddles and a white ute. I get out as soon as Nicola yanks the handbrake. The detective, who'd stayed twenty metres behind us the whole way, is on her feet nearly as fast as I am. She points at the ute. *Is that his?*

I nod. Beyond I can see the wooden steps and handrail that mark the start of the trail, and before I can think too hard about it my feet are falling down those steps, past the information signs and picnic area, wanting this to be over, all of it. Nicola is there with me. The detective is behind her, muttering and panting.

Down we trudge.

The trees cluster, rising high, then thin out, giving way to a maze of ferns. Small bracken-like ferns that scrape our legs; carpets of ferns that spread across fallen logs; squat ferns; slender ferns; tree ferns that must be three metres tall, with great canopies of fronds that splay out above us, blanking out the sky. And all of them green, deep green, and the lower the wending path takes us, the deeper those shades of green become.

After ten minutes of trudging we start hearing it: the knocking. A monotonous, heavy metronome of sound, coming from somewhere below us. I turn to Nicola and the detective. On their faces I see the same things I am feeling: confusion, apprehension and tinges of exhaustion. *What's that?* Nicola asks, and I can only shrug. The knocking continues.

We keep walking, drawn down by the noise.

After a while—five, ten, thirty minutes; I don't know— the ground flattens out. We have reached the low heart of Notley. The path runs adjacent to the small, sloshing creek I can remember from my childhood. Its gurgles are loud, but not loud enough to drown out the knocking, which is closer now, calling to us from the middle distance ahead. We keep following the trail, the knocks. Soon we are led into a flat grove, where the ferns are not so thick, and all of them are of the towering tree-fern variety. A small bridge chops the stream. We step across it and begin threading our way through the strange behemoths.

And then we find it: the source of the sound.

I was wrong: they aren't knocks at all. They are chops. An axe is being heaved into the trunk of one of the tree ferns in an even, methodical rhythm. Its blade is biting into the fibrous trunk, spraying out stringy chunks of vegetation. The fronds shake and spray dew each time the blade lands. That's the sound we can hear: the felling of tree ferns.

The axe is being swung by Levi.

It is cold down here, but he isn't wearing a shirt. The pile of tree-fern logs stacked a few metres from where he is standing goes a way to explaining this, but still: he must be freezing. His shirt is lying on a sawhorse near the logs, along with some kind of furry hat or bag. Sweat pops on his pale skin. He does not look healthy. He has always been slender, but now he is emaciated. His ribs slant out at harsh angles, and the skin on his cheeks and collarbone has sunk into pockets below the bone. And the change does not end with his flesh—his hair, usually so neat, is long and knotted, spraying out from his scalp in greasy tufts.

I have been so angry with him. But now all I feel is a rushing tide of worry.

Nicola and the detective make sounds—gasps, I think, or just short breaths—but they don't say anything. He hasn't seen us yet; the axe is still swinging and biting. I walk towards him, and still he doesn't see me until I say: *Levi.*

His body jerks with sudden violence. His head snaps towards us. There is no recognition in his eyes. I keep talking. *What are you doing?*

He stares at me. Huffing chest. Sweaty face. Narrow, red-streaked eyes. *Charlotte.* He repeats my name, as if reminding himself. *Charlotte.* His voice is thin. *You're back.*

*Yeah.* I focus on my breathing, keeping measured, keeping still.

He lowers the axe. *I was worried about you.*

*I'm fine.* There is more to say, so much more, questions and accusations and concerns and pleas, but in this dank moment, in this dim, special place, I can't get my words right. And now his narrow face has been broken apart by a

205

huge, manic smile. His once-white teeth, always meticulously scrubbed, are covered in a grey-green film. His eyes are whipping around the grove.

*I knew you'd be okay.* He gestures at the axe, the sawhorse, the fern logs. *I'm sorry—I've been a bit preoccupied.* Finally he looks at Nicola and the detective. *Who are they?*

Again I pace my breaths. Again I stay calm and cold. I lie a flat palm out in front of Nicola. *This is my friend Nicola.* Then I indicate the detective. *And this is—well, you know her. You hired her to find me.*

His stare swings back to me. The smile has fallen, and his hand drops down to grab the furry object on the sawhorse, which he lifts to his chest. *No. I don't think so.*

Now the detective is stepping forward, saying: *I'm getting paid whether you recognise me or not.* But he's already turned away from us to frown at the fern he'd been attacking as we arrived. His fingers are clenching and unclenching the fur.

I ask again. *Levi, what are doing?*

He looks back up. *Oh. Yes.* He gestures at the stack of logs with his axe. *I'm building you a coffin.*

*I don't need a coffin.* Now, when the heat builds and bubbles, is when I need to stay calm. More than ever; more than anything. *I don't want a coffin.*

He raises the axe. *No, not yet.* It thunks into the wounded tree fern. *But eventually you will.*

*No, I won't.* I start walking towards him. Slow steps. *Let's go home, Levi.*

*You will!* In a pale flash he spins around—fast, rigid, as if every movement is a sudden thought. *You just haven't thought about it. If you're buried in a coffin, you won't be cremated. You won't come back.* He waves the furry object. *You won't have to go through it.*

It is as if he is trying to coax the flames out of me. Yet he can't know—can he? It is so cold, so wet, and I am filled with so much heat. *You're not making sense*, I tell him.

His fingers shake as they burrow deeper into the fur. *I'm doing it for you.*

*I don't know what you're doing, Levi.* The stream keeps gurgling. I want to dive into it. *Why are you even down here?*

He blinks. *Mum loved this place.* He looks up at the canopy. *It seemed right.*

I take a gamble; with heat pulsing beneath my nails, I reach out. *It's not. But it's okay.* My palm lands on his naked shoulder. *We need to leave. I'll find you some help.*

He looks at my hand. *I don't need help. I'm helping you.*

*Please, Levi. You can help me by coming with me.*

*You don't understand.*

My hands grips. *Levi. We're leaving.* I shouldn't do it; I should let him go; but he is stoking my anger, and he does need help, and he is the only family I have left, and now I am pulling at his shoulder. He stumbles off balance, as if he isn't used to how frail he has become, and slaps at my arm with the hand that is clutching the furry thing. I lift my free hand to grab at his, but instead I end up with a fistful of the golden-brown fur.

His eyes fly wide. *Let go of that.*

There is warmth in the fur, warmth different from the heat inside me. Where mine burns, this glows.

He is shrieking now. *It's mine!* And now we are both pulling at the fur. It's childish, and reckless, but I need to help him, and we need to get out of here, and I don't want to let go of this golden warmth. Suddenly Nicola is lunging at the axe hanging in Levi's other hand. She grabs it and yanks, hard. We are all thrown off balance. But none of us lets go.

Levi looks down at Nicola as she clutches the axe. He swings the handle with a strength that belies his hungry frame, and Nicola is thrown backwards. She crashes into the sawhorse. Her head hits the timber, and the sick crack of bone on wood rings loud. She slumps. Her eyes roll high. And then she is still, but I am not. The bent mess of her body flicks my mind white. Thoughts and plans are chased away by the heat I no longer have the will to contain. I rise; I roar; I rip the fur from Levi's hand.

He shrieks again, and jumps forward to snatch it back. But he is too late; the fur is already burning.

I let the flames fly from beneath my nails, and releasing them is an exquisite relief. The tip of each of my fingers feels like a swollen dam, bursting and draining free. The fur sucks the flames into its fibre, smoking and sizzling in my grasp. Levi is screaming, high and horrible, like a kicked child, but he cannot come near me, for my flames are too hot and huge. They are pouring out my ears now, and my nose, and streaming out of my eyes in great blue rivers. From my toenails they are leaping, from my navel they are bursting, and from between my legs they are crackling, tides and floods I cannot control. Everywhere they are rushing out, and everywhere the heat is wild and glorious.

It must be wondrous to see.

Over the whooshing flames I can just make out my brother's screams. He sounds like a distant whistle. I look down to see him tearing at his face with uncut nails, his eyes fixed on the fur in my hand. Unlike my blue flames, the fur is burning purple. A great plume of smoke is rising from its centre. The hairs fizz and spit, releasing far more energy than should be possible.

But the fury of these little flames mean nothing to me. I watch as the pelt burns out. The last of its violet tongues die in my palm, and its final wisps of smoke rise into the night. I throw the ash onto the dirt. Levi falls to his knees and begins scraping it into a little black mound.

I stand over him, allowing my flames to send delicate shudders through my skin. Then I see Nicola lying by the sawhorse. I remember the sound of her head hitting the wood. She still isn't moving.

I step towards her, but as soon as I move I hear a yelp. I look down and see Levi writhing in the dirt. Blue flames have run across the dead vegetation and are licking at his bare chest. I step away from him, and as I do I can see more flames spreading out across the grove around me. They are marching through the moss; they are lapping over the axe handle; they are climbing up the tree ferns. The more I move, the more drops of fire I shake free from my body. I turn back to Nicola. The detective is at her side now, helping her up. Levi is scurrying towards his pile of fern logs. The flames are rising higher.

I close my eyes. I try to cool, to calm, to kill the burn, but I can't. The flames keep gushing.

And then it hits me. Not a thought, but a force. Something strong and fast.

Nicola.

She smashes into my torso, pushing me to the ground. I open my eyes and see her face inches from my own. Her mouth is a tight grimace. I try to push her off, but she is holding me down. Her knees are on my chest and her hands are wrapped around my wrists. The sparks in my nails halt, but fire is still streaming out of my mouth, my eyes, everywhere.

I see tongues of it lapping over her hands and forearms. But she does not let go.

Agony wrenches her face. And she does not let go.

I struggle, I buck, I try to yell, but she won't let me up. Not until my flames have stopped. And eventually they do, as they always do when she holds me. Under her touch I can feel the coals in my stomach smoulder and die, and as they do the fire ceases to flow. My head swims and flips, as if I've just fallen from a great height.

Nicola falls off me. I blink and gasp, and slowly roll over. When I do, I see that the detective is dragging Nicola by her feet towards the little stream. She dumps her in the water and starts splashing more of it over her arms. I stand up; I need to help; she is hurt; but I can't stay on my feet. I am woozy and hollow, and my limbs have no strength. All I can do is moan her name, but she doesn't hear me. Or if she does, she doesn't look up. The detective throws more water. I can't see Nicola's face.

On the other side of the grove Levi is sitting with his knees drawn up to his chest, watching the fire dance around him. There is terror and confusion on his face. I start crawling in his direction, trying to say something. It's only after a few lunges that I realise it would be impossible for him to hear me above the flames, for they are now monstrous. Their blueness has given way to regular orange-red fury, and they are climbing high, taking hold in every branch, frond and scrap of fuel.

It takes the fire changing colour for me to realise it: we aren't leaving here. Our ash will join our mother's.

Back at the stream the detective is still cupping water over Nicola. She hasn't seen how large the fire has grown. Or if she has, she is denying it, preferring to spend her last minutes helping to ease Nicola's pain. I lie my face against hot soil and try to remember everything I have loved, everything I have treasured, but I am so tired, and the images won't hold. My fit has left me hollow. All I can think of is how much I want Nicola to live. I stare at the flames approaching the stream, wishing they would shrink or go out, wanting only to have had the strength to send her away before we ever came here; to have told her to leave me forever, back at the house. I am crying now: tears or fire, I don't know. I will the flames down, knowing it won't do anything.

Yet, in the gushing face of the flames, I see something. They are shrinking. I am sure of it.

Not all the flames. Not the high, surging fires that are spreading out from the grove; just the ones surrounding us, here by the stream. They are crackling down into glowing embers. The detective keeps splashing, noticing nothing. Neither does Levi; he is rocking back and forth, curled in a ball. Only I see the flames recede into smoking coals. And only I see the man step out of them.

He smiles at me. I've heard people say that they can never remember what he looks like, or that he's hard to describe, as if he has no defining features. But I've always found his smile unforgettable; when I think of him it's always the first thing I see. His mouth skewing into a friendly arc while his eyes stay flat and cold. The sadness in these eyes: sadness that touches despair. His lips spread but do not open, a taut mask of happiness, while the sorrow leaks like tears or blood. He is smiling like this now. Small among the ferns. Lonely in the flames.

I am dreaming. I must be. Or I am hallucinating, or I am dead. My father doesn't seem to care. He mouths something to me and holds a hand over his chest. Then he looks up, into the sky, and releases a long, heavy sigh. His eyes are closed.

That's when the rain starts falling. First in small, hazy drops, then in a steady pitter-patter, and finally in huge swamping sheets. The remains of the fire are swiftly washed out. I wipe water from my eyes: my father has disappeared. A patch of mud gurgles in the spot where he'd stood. And now the rain, first so welcome, tries to drown us.

# CLOUD

And how furious was that rain—how brutally did it lash the green gorge! How much rage and angst and sorrow was contained in those sheets of winter water! How much of herself did that cloud pour into her storm!

As she smelt the smoke her fog body flinched, her wind voice screamed, her wisp eyes streamed, and in those sprinting streams was every scrap of thought she owned: every splinter of memory; every puff of pain; every big and powerful part of herself, swelling each drop and propelling it downwards with sky-high force.

The rain hit Notley first, zeroing in on the smoke. From the ferns it spread outwards, across farms, roads and forests and the nearby Tamar, where it overpowered the salinity and bloated the banks. Down the fattened river the storm rolled, to the levees of Launceston, which collapsed beneath the heaving waves. The flat northern suburbs were instantly flooded. The storm kept raging, the river kept rising, and the rest of the city soon gave way to the unwelcome wetness as well. So too did its gorge: water climbed up its rocky walls and its forested foothills turned into the world's strangest reef. It was a place accustomed to flooding, but not like this: not from this direction, not this violently.

The cloud's rage howled on, pushing the storm east and west, north and south. Fields became bogs; ponds became lakes; wombats swam like water rats, and water rats cavorted like seals, drunk on the storm's power. A muscly current turned Tunbridge into Nobridge. The Avoca post office was washed clean of all its letters. Hours after it broke over Notley, the storm reached the southern capital's sprawling suburbs. It lashed the huddled houses before pouring onto the shiny docks, where fortunes of yachts clattered against weathered concrete. Hulls caved; masts snapped; engines died. Catamarans dived to the harbour floor.

And there was more, for the storm was not finished. It pushed further south, down past Kingston and into the sleepy Huon. After another day of raging it made it all the way to lonely Melaleuca, where its howling torrents filled an abandoned tin mine to its jagged brim, sending a colony of cormorants reeling up into the sky. Something else reeled out of the mine, too: something foul and broken, limp and swollen, something built with flesh and feathers, yet pulsing with a thirst that no amount of rainwater could slake. By the time the storm passed it was floating on the rising face of Bathurst Harbour, heading out to the ocean. Yet was there a flicker of movement in its violent black feathers? Did its waxy nose-bill rise up from the water? Did its mangled wings begin carving through the water, dragging its body towards land?

Only the cloud could have seen. And she was too busy weeping.

On she went, on with her tantrums and wind-screams. Valleys became basins; orchards became lap pools; snakes shed their skins and morphed into slime-skinned eels. But why all this dreadful drenching? Why was the storm so monstrous and severe?

The answer lay in the curls of the smoke that first rose from the Notley fire. Not fern smoke; not tree smoke; not even the rich fatty flavour of flesh smoke. No—it was the smoke that fizzed out of a small, golden-brown pelt in the heart of the fire. A special pelt: a river pelt. A pelt that had belonged to the other half of the cloud's heart. The pelt of her waterlocked love—a love that had recently disappeared after centuries of mutual, touchless adoration.

It had been weeks since she'd felt his eyes gazing up at her from the river and, despite her knowledge of his divinity, she had feared the worst. The fur smoke that rose into her wisps and wafts from Notley confirmed it: he was dead. She would never mistake that scent. He who owned the river now burned in the flames. Never again would he climb the dark mountain and stare up in hopeful worship. Never again would she feed his kingdom with her tears of lonesome love. No more would she nourish him with her rain. No more; not ever.

A cloud's sorrow: you cannot imagine it. But you can feel it, whenever a storm hits the world with uncommon force. When mountains crack and forests flood. When rivers surge and oceans bloat. When there is no true shelter left in the world. For the hardest storms are made of sorrow.

Such sorrow came to the island, and tried to drown it.

# SEA

I have always been afraid of the ocean. This fear comes from my father, I think—he wouldn't even dip a toe in a tide pool. When we were children I would wander on the beach, Charlotte would tumble in the waves and he would wait at the edge of the gully, keeping an eye on us without ever stepping onto the sand. We never asked him about it. There wouldn't have been any point: he wasn't the kind of man who answered questions like that.

When he left we kept going down to the beach, as if nothing had changed, but on our sun-smacked backs we could feel the absence of his eyes. And when I first turned to see the fatherless edge of the gully, I felt the fear shiver through me, as if it had been transferred from his mind to my own. Charlotte was out in the water, crashing her shoulders into a breaking wave, and the ocean's weight, strangeness and malice were suddenly revealed to me. I have not touched saltwater since.

Or at least, I hadn't until I splashed my foot as I climbed into Karl's dinghy, three days after the fire at Notley. I'd forgotten how cold the ocean was. How quickly it soaked through to the skin; how stubbornly it refused to dry. I didn't say anything to Karl. I figured it wouldn't have been news to him.

How I'd ended up in his boat: a combination of my sister, his daughter, and my folly.

Δ

The morning after the fire I woke up in my bed, with a few small burns shining across my body and no idea how I'd got there. Charlotte later told me that the detective I'd hired months earlier had carried me to her car and driven me home. She was no longer there—she'd left that night, apparently, muttering about gin and cats and sandwiches, although she'd promised to return and collect the money I owed her. I barely remembered hiring this detective; of her dragging me out of a fire I remembered even less.

Then, in the low light of the morning, my sister told me more.

How the fire had been quenched by the biggest storm in decades, maybe centuries.

How floods now stretched all across the island, from the wide north coast to the southwest plains.

How our father had appeared, as if from nowhere, before disappearing again when the flames went out.

How furious she was.

How she hoped my wounds hurt.

How her friend, Nicola, wore burns far worse than my own.

I can remember what happened, but it's like remembering a dream, or a story I'd overheard. I knew what I had done, but I couldn't believe I'd done it. My clearest memory was of the pelt I'd taken from Hough, and the strange, swelling confidence that had pulsed through me the longer I kept it in my grasp. Now that it was gone I felt much less sure of myself, but my thoughts were clearer, and I no longer felt compelled to follow every thought and desire that welled up within me.

But it wasn't just the pelt; even before then, when I'd been pursuing my coffin plan, my memories were murky, as if they were someone else's that had been carefully recited to me. I consider myself a rational person, but my actions since our mother died weren't all that rational. Nor was the way I'd treated my sister. Thinking about it was confusing, and filled me with a sickening shame. I tried telling myself that even though my behaviour was wrong, my intentions were right—but was that even true? Did I really have what was best for Charlotte in the heart of my plans?

The truth: I had been erratic, selfish and weak. I had failed her when she needed me most.

Charlotte left me lying in the bed, where I stayed for

another hour, chasing these thoughts around in circles. When I got up I could think of nothing else to do but ask for her forgiveness, although I knew I didn't deserve it. I could tell she was still angry, but she said that she would forgive me, probably, in time. She was holding a mug. The tea inside it was roiling with frothy, milk-brown bubbles—almost as if it was boiling. I was going to say something, I don't know what, when she told me: *As long as you forgive me too.*

I have nothing to forgive. I have only trust to win back. But she has always been smarter than me: one day, I might understand what she means.

Δ

It was Nicola who suggested the dinghy. We had gone to see her at the hospital that afternoon. Charlotte hadn't wanted me to come, but I insisted. I couldn't do much for Nicola's injuries, but I could apologise. After a brief argument, Charlotte had relented. We didn't speak much on the way there, other than to comment on the smashed trees, huge puddles and debris that the storm had scattered across the landscape. The wreckage was everywhere. I had never seen a spectacle of natural destruction. Roofs had been ripped off houses, and whole forests seemed to have been uprooted and thrown in random directions. Great pools of floodwater lay across every remotely flat field. It almost made me sorry that I could not remember it happening. But then I remembered the fire.

I'm not an imaginative person, nor am I usually pessimistic, but I had been convinced that Nicola would be unconscious and wrapped in swathes of cotton like a mummy. She was just lying in a white bed with simple bandages adorning her forearms. Trees were bending outside a narrow window. I hovered in the doorway, not sure what to do or say, as Charlotte hurried to the bed. Nicola kept her arms flat as my sister buffeted her with a heavy embrace, but a smile stretched out her lips and a red wave washed beneath the skin on her cheeks. Charlotte was whispering fast words that I couldn't make out. After a few seconds she pulled back to look at Nicola's arms. Their foreheads fell to rest against one another. More words were muttered, by both of them.

I am not good at these things, but I began to understand, I think.

So did Nicola's family, who were sitting in stiff chairs in the corner of the room. They—I assumed they were her mother, father and sister—were all wearing expressions of quiet surprise. I cleared my throat and said hello; though they responded politely, I could tell they were much more interested in what was going on between their daughter and my sister.

Greetings and introductions followed. It seemed that Nicola had told them about Charlotte, or at least mentioned her to them, because they greeted her with vague tones of recognition and gratitude. Of me, however, they remained wary, and did not move from the other side of the room. Which I understood.

With their eyes on me—or the ground, in the case of Nicola's sister—I began what I'd gone there to do: apologise.

But it didn't go the way I'd been rehearsing in my head. I started by saying *pain* and *sorry* and *I didn't mean* but the words didn't come out the right way, or in the right order. I kept talking. Normally I keep my sentences short, if I say anything at all, but in this small hospital room I began babbling to the point of incomprehension. I said things like *intentions* and *make it better* and *please* and *hurt* and *never again* and *never wanted to*; but the faster I spoke, the less sense I made. They were all staring at me now, and when I saw Charlotte's eyes casting confusion towards me my stream of words gave way to a single, ragged sob. A sob that choked into a howl.

I had not cried since I was a small child—not even at our mother's cremation. But now my howl was joined by a rapid gurgle of other sobs, and tears, and the occasional moan. I didn't know what was happening to me; I tried to maintain my composure, but failed; I failed as badly as I'd failed my sister. Somehow I ended up on the squeaky floor at the foot of the bed. My throat ached. I was punching the linoleum. Someone was rubbing my shoulder.

It was in this moment, or sometime around it, that Nicola had her idea.

Δ

Two days later I was squelching water against my sock as her father motored us over the grey waves. I'd expected it to be a rough and jolting ride, but the dinghy cut smoothly across the water. I clung onto the edge anyway. I don't think Karl noticed how scared I was. If he did, he ignored it.

*There's no point*, I'd heard him say in the hospital. *The stocks are too thin. You can't make a career out of it anymore.* Nicola held his hand from her bed. *That doesn't matter, Dad. Please. Just do this for him.* She looked at Charlotte. *For me.*

I didn't know what it was that he was supposed to be doing, for me or for his daughter, and the last place I wanted to be was out at sea with a grumpy fisherman. But Charlotte had agreed with Nicola's plan. When we got back from the hospital she stared me in the eyes, a stare of fury and concern, and told me I should go with Karl. So I did. And I didn't ask any questions.

We pushed past the Hawley heads, and the smooth ride I'd been almost enjoying took on a lurching lilt. The boat rose and thumped beneath me in uneven strides. I focused on the beach that was receding from sight, and its whiteness, and the green-beige smudge of bluegums that rose behind it. I began worrying about seasickness, storms, tsunamis, until Karl suddenly switched off the engine.

I turned from the horizon to see him throwing an anchor over the side. A chain rattled out behind it. It plunged down, disappearing into the dark water. *What happens now?* I asked.

Karl threw something black and flappy towards me. I caught it on my chest. *Put this on*, he said.

*I'm getting in the water?*

*Yep.*

I shook my head. *No. No, thanks. I don't think I want to do that.*

*Suit yourself.* He sat down on the small bench in the

middle of the dinghy and pulled a paperback out of his jacket. *This was a waste of time, then.*

I looked down at the wetsuit. It felt plush and thick. *Why do I have to get in the water? What happens then?*

Karl didn't look up from his book. *Just do it, mate.*

Charlotte's face swam into my head, and the stare she'd given when we'd returned home from the hospital. I unbuttoned my jacket, peeled off my shirt and pants and socks, and started climbing into the suit. Its fabric fought my body at every opportunity. Karl had to help me force my limbs through the holes. Eventually I was in. The stretchy neoprene clung to me, and I felt constricted, even though I could breathe with ease. Karl yanked the zip on my back up to the base of my neck and handed me a pair of flippers. *These go on your feet.* He sat back down with his book. *You go in the water.*

I had more questions, but there didn't seem much point in asking them. I wedged my feet into the flippers, dangled my legs over the boat and, with a burst of resolve that I hadn't felt since I'd gripped Hough's golden-brown pelt, launched myself into the ocean.

It wasn't as cold as I'd expected. This was probably due to the wetsuit, which was also helping me to float. I looked up at Karl, waiting for an instruction. He was pointing towards a patch of darker water, ten or fifteen metres away. *Go over there.*

I paddled over to the patch. *What now?*

*Wait.*

*For what?*

*Just wait.*

I kicked at the water beneath me, trying not to think about sharks and jellyfish and giant squid. Thanks to the wetsuit it was easy to keep my head above water, but after ten minutes my legs were beginning to tire.

*How long do I have to do this?*

Karl didn't respond. He was still reading.

I kept kicking, seeing nothing, gradually becoming colder. Ten more minutes passed. I asked again: *How much longer?*

Karl didn't look up from his page. *As long as it takes.*

I resolved to not ask any more questions, not unless I was drowning. I would stay out here as long as he made me. This was probably the point of the trip, I realised. To teach me patience. Or respect. Or humility. I kicked and floated on, as the waves began rolling higher and my legs began aching in a deep, listless way.

I had fallen into a kind of numb trance when water sloshed over my bottom lip. I spat it out and realised my neck had stiffened with cold. I tried to straighten my head, but I couldn't. More water lapped into my mouth, salty and insistent. *Karl*, I yelped, *I can't do this anymore. I'm exhausted.*

Still he did not look up. *You're nearly done.*

*I've learnt my lesson. I have. I'm going to drown.*

*You're not here for a lesson, mate.* He finally put his book down and gestured behind me. *You're here for him.*

I turned, awkward and heavy, following the line of his arm. Something was there, but I was too slow to see it before it splashed back underwater. Fear surged through me. I pivoted, kicking wildly. *Steady*, Karl barked. I wanted to shout something back at him, something harsh and crude, but I was too tired, too cold. And before I could think of anything, the splashing figure re-emerged, half a metre from my face.

It was a seal. A pup. Its head was small, brown and sleek, and great wiry whiskers forked out from beside its wet black nose. A fishy stench hit my open mouth like a slap, and I nearly gagged. *Easy*, I heard Karl yell. *Go easy*.

I breathed through my nose as the pup studied me with its huge, glimmering eyes.

Karl called out again. *Give him your hand.*

I was beyond thinking, beyond surprise; all I could do was obey. I took my right hand from the water and held it in front of the seal. The waves were rolling higher now, and harder, and I was struggling to keep my head above the water. The pup kept looking at me. I spat water. My legs went limp.

I kept my hand high.

And then, as I began to slide beneath the sea, the pup rested its face on my palm. Its huge wet eyes bored into mine. A puff of fish breath blew out of its nose. Something ballooned inside me, something huge and uncontainable, from the pit of my stomach to the back of my throat. As it expanded I rose up, high on the wake. And in that rising moment I held on to the seal, and kept my eyes locked on his, and waited to fall back beneath the waves.

But out there in the salt, that something kept swelling. It has kept me afloat ever since.

## NOTE

*Flames* is—obviously, I think—a work of fiction. The writing of it, however, was influenced by a few people, places and events that should be acknowledged. The lives of Deny King, Marjorie Bligh and Taffy the Bee Man (Helmer Henry Hastings Huxley) all served as inspiration for various characters, while the Launceston floods of 2016 and the Dunalley bushfire of 2013 inspired certain events in the story. More broadly, anyone who has travelled south of the Australian mainland may recognise some of the history, geography, flora and fauna in this book. Or they may recognise nothing at all; I have made up a lot of strange things here. It's all I know how to do.

*Robbie Arnott, Hobart, February 2018*

## ACKNOWLEDGMENTS

There is simply no way this book would exist without the support of the following people: David Winter, Ben Walter, Adam Ouston, Rachel Edwards, Julia Carlomagno and the person I love most in the world, Emily Bill. Thank you all, so very much, for all your help, guidance, advice and support.

Thank you also to everyone at Text, for believing in this book and helping it make its way into the world.

Finally, I would like to thank the people who have supported not just this book, but everything I have ever written: my mother Chris, my father Geoff, my sister Jenny and my brother Scott. I may not always be the greatest son or brother, but you are the best family I could ever ask for.

NOTE: Emily has insisted that I also acknowledge our cat, Zelda, who stalked, headbutted and generally harassed me during almost every moment I was writing this book. So, bad luck, Zelda—your efforts to thwart me have failed.